COLD MOON
HONOR

COLD MOON HONOR

•

LAURI OLSEN

AVALON BOOKS
THOMAS BOUREGY AND COMPANY, INC.
401 LAFAYETTE STREET
NEW YORK, NEW YORK 10003

FIRST PRINTING

PRINTED IN THE UNITED STATES OF AMERICA
ON ACID-FREE PAPER
BY HADDON CRAFTSMEN, BLOOMSBURG, PENNSYLVANIA

Dedicated
with love to
Francis Dean Hancock,
good Indian,
best friend,
cherished memory

Acknowledgments

The author extends sincere thanks to: Helga Pac, Montana
Department of Fish, Wildlife and Parks; Victor Singer and Mark
Bruised Head, of the Crow Tribe; Tom Big Spring, of the
Blackfoot Tribe; and Robert Edgar Olsen, Logging Consultant.

Chapter One

At daybreak, jagged McAllister Peak loomed cold and purple against the awakening Montana sky. Snow obliterated the timberline of the mountain, caping it in a vesture of white like a corpulent robed monarch.

Terra Bartlett pulled off the highway and squinted up at the majestic summit. In the faltering light of dawn, the mountain was quiet. The tracks of big game animals traversing the mountain to drink in the ice-gorged river were a frozen testament to their winter residence. Trailing into the tall pines, the tracks in the snow crisscrossed the thickly forested hillside. The stillness, the overwhelming serenity of the mountains in the early morning, was palpable even from the cab of her truck.

Crimson striations in the cloud cover signaled the dawn of a day without wind.

Good, she thought. *We need a calm day.*

There'd been enough blowing snow already this winter to make life miserable for everybody. This had been the kind of winter the old-timers reminisced about. Roads drifted in. Plumbing pipes froze. Wind-chill factors plummeted. People grew ornery from the constant, howling gales.

The stress of foraging in deep snowdrifts was beginning to show on wildlife throughout the region. Bison at the Whispering Water Range wore bruised noses, the result of butting through ice-crusted snow for their meager grass re-

1

wards. White-tailed deer in the canyon grew rangy looking. Elk were getting scrawny and ribby.

Yes, it was time for a calm day.

The young woman slid out of her pickup and trudged around the front of the cab, her heavy pacs crunching in the hard snow. Without four-wheel drive, the truck wouldn't attain the traction necessary to reach the elk's winter range on the far side of the mountain.

Twisting the freezing metal knobs, she locked the wheel hubs into position. Her breath fanned white and crystalline as she pulled the collar of her uniform jacket more closely around her neck. As a Game Management Officer for the Montana Department of Fish, Wildlife & Parks, she had to be prepared for all types of weather. In the intense heat of high-altitude summer days, as well as the biting subzero cold of a Montana January, Terra knew that when she spent the day working big game, she had to dress comfortably, according to the weather. Sunburn and frostbite were constant menaces.

Today, however, the danger of windburn seemed unlikely. For that she was thankful. The thermometer at her condo had read four below zero this morning when she left for work.

Squaring her pile-lined hat, she climbed into the driver's seat and fired the truck into action.

All four wheels dug in, climbing slowly to navigate the mountain on a series of switchbacks. At the first clearing, she rolled to a stop, set the parking brake, and stepped out.

"Good morning, Wheezer!" Her voice carried easily in the frigid mountain air.

In his brown padded coveralls, Wheezer Johannson looked like an overgrown gingerbread cookie. His hard hat, dented and paint-chipped, sat precariously atop a knitted liner that covered his ears and fastened under his chin.

Nobody called him Earl Harold Johannson. The legacy left from too many years of sucking on cigarettes had determined his nickname. He hadn't smoked for six years now; still, the moniker persisted.

The logger's grin spread across his face and shot a twinkle into his eyes. Setting his oil-spattered chainsaw aside, he plodded to the truck.

"Howdy, Terra!"

"Hi, buddy," she acknowledged him with a broad smile. "Your skidder start okay this morning?" When the temperature hovered near zero, the logging equipment's diesel fuel turned to gel. If equipment didn't start, a day's work, and thus a day's pay, would be lost.

The log harvest on the mountain had enabled local sawmills to extricate dying and diseased wood from an otherwise healthy timber stand. It was a necessary part of the life cycle of the forest. Wheezer Johannson was a third-generation Montana logger; his familiarity in the woods was coupled with his respect for the land. He logged the selected area efficiently, leaving no long-term impact on the forest.

"She started hard." The logger shrugged, with a nod of his graying head toward the huge tractor used to pull logs from the cutting site. "But she'll be okay now."

"Same with my truck," Terra agreed. "He was cold this morning, even with the headbolt heater in him, but he's purring now."

"Where you headed?"

The young woman yanked a thumb toward the road. "Up by Hannon Pass. We're radio-collaring elk today."

The winter elk range, across the mountain from the logging site, was most easily accessible over roads built by the lumber company. In her three years with the FWP Service, Terra had become a familiar sight bouncing over the rutted logging roads in her brown pickup with the government logo on its doors. Along the way, she had become acquainted with many of the land users. Wheezer was one of her favorites.

"I'd better let you get back to work. The crew should

be up ahead waiting for me,'' she continued. ''Take care, Wheezer.''

Her thick, raven black braid flipped over one shoulder as she turned. Wheezer reached out and yanked it gently.

''Be careful on that road, young'un,'' he cautioned her. At twenty-seven, she was the same age as his youngest daughter. Wheezer never tried to hide his paternal attitude toward her. He liked the bright-eyed Native American woman.

Deep down inside, though, Wheezer Johannson didn't believe being a Game Management Officer was woman's work. It was long hours in extreme temperatures. The work was physically demanding and mentally challenging.

But, he had to admit, she never stopped being a woman. She never resorted to cussing or power plays to gain male acceptance as one of them. If anything, the men on her crew respected her more for that.

Wheezer recognized the dedication Terra Bartlett had to the wildlife of the Big Sky Country. She did her job well. He admired that in any person.

The huge bull elk shifted his massive head from left to right, wary eyes surveying the whitened expanse of meadow. An immense rack of horns pointed forward as the animal lowered his nose, pawed the ground, and threw his head back again.

As exalted leader, the bull had assumed his place guiding the herd. The powerful animals, elegant beasts the Indians called wapiti, wound out of the canyon and pushed their way through the deep snow blanketing the frozen native grasses.

Now, he sniffed the air suspiciously, nostrils flared, as the herd line neared service trucks waiting at the meadow's perimeter. The bull's muscles rippled, then flinched as he bolted from formation and bounded through the snow. The scent of danger permeated his world.

Overhead in the distance, the FWP-rented helicopter

swooped into the canyon mouth, its whirring blades cutting the silence of the mountains with a discordant, echoing clatter. The pilot dropped to his position above the herd and hung suspended against the sky like a bobbing puppet.

Hooves thundered against the frozen ground as the herd galloped, full speed, in frenzied confusion. Snorting and puffing, they scattered across the meadow. In attempting to elude the game officers, the herd veered north. Within this shadow of the mountains, snow seldom melted before July. This early in January, drifts three feet deep hampered the animals' movements.

Terra and her colleagues braced themselves. The animals would unwittingly play into their hands within seconds.

"Pull him in!" a senior game officer yelled.

"Watch him!"

"Heads up!" Terra's warning rang out as the bull elk, snorting and enraged, neared the workers.

Huge nets yawned at the end of the meadow, awaiting their prey. The staff were on alert, watching the animal's every move.

Swinging forward, the helicopter herded the bull toward the service area. Clattering closer and closer to the survey station, the rotocraft lifted into the sky at the last possible moment, its mission accomplished.

"Get him . . ."

"Bring him in!" Frank Daniel's instruction echoed against the hillside. Instantly, the net collapsed over the powerful animal. His front legs buckled. Horns tangled in the netting. Thrashing wildly within the net, the bull relinquished control only when the game officers subdued him by throwing themselves bodily against his shoulders and flanks. His breath was labored, distinctively hollow sounding. His sides heaved.

"He's a big 'un," Frank panted. Wrestling the bull elk to the ground, even within the confining net, was a job requiring teamwork from all five workers. They had only a moment to assess the huge critter before the routine of collaring began.

The elk's hide was in good shape. The herd had obviously wintered well, despite the deep snow. His weight was good, his muscles strong and defined. No sign of dehydration wrinkled his pliant skin.

"You're not going to be needing these old things, fella." Don Lee's voice was smooth as he prepared to de-horn the animal. Some bulls had already lost their horns by this time of the winter; this particular specimen still sported the massive rack that had failed to slough off naturally. With no blood supply to the old horns, the procedure was painless to the animal and afforded an additional degree of safety to the game survey crew. Come spring, the bull would start growing another impressive rack.

"Bring his nose around," Pam Craft requested. She squinted against the early-morning sun reflecting off the snow. Grabbing the bull's muzzle carefully but firmly, she used one thumb to slide the elk's lips up to its gumline. "Let's get a look at those teeth and see how old you are, big guy."

As he readied a syringe for a blood sample, Pat Bohardt shifted his knee against the elk's flank. A twenty-year veteran of the department, Pat could handle big game with his eyes closed. His respect for the animal was apparent as he set about his tasks quickly, efficiently. The sample blood, when tested back at the state's veterinary research lab, would screen for any diseases in the herd. Grabbing the scruff of the animal's neck, Pat plunged the needle in and withdrew the blood sample.

"Ready for tagging?" he called over his shoulder.

"Let's go." Pam held a numbered tag in each hand.

Terra readied the radio collar.

The ear tags were clicked into place, one on either side of the enormous head. Encircling the animal's neck, the radio collar was positioned; it would enable the game of-

ficers to track the elk's migration in the coming months
through radio signals.

The immense bull, with the infinite beauty only a wild
animal possessed, was remarkably docile throughout the
process.

"Using the nets surely beats tranquilizing them," Terra
remarked.

"It's the only way to go," Frank agreed. He stepped
back, pulling the net from the animal and allowing it to
kick free. Instantly, the huge animal rolled from its side
and maneuvered its powerful legs to stand. Loping cau-
tiously across the service area, the bull returned to the herd
in the distance. Its head was proudly erect.

Throughout the morning, and late into the afternoon, the
program continued. The random sampling, representing the
entire herd, was guided into nets and processed with blood
sample collection, tags, and collars.

"Must be going toward four-thirty." Pam stretched her
back and searched the sky for fleeting sunlight. The mountains would be in total darkness by five o'clock.

"I'm ready to start back down the mountain." Frank
retrieved his gear from the site and began loading his truck.

"Pam, how would you like to ride back down the mountain with me?" Terra longed for company. It had been an
exhausting day, and what didn't ache or feel cold on her
was covered in mud and elk hair. *Just another day in Par-
adise,* she mused.

"You bet. Let me get my lunch pail and I'll let Frank
know I'm going back down with you."

"Thank goodness it's Friday night," Pam reminded her
coworker as their truck wound down the mountain road.

"Big plans for the weekend?"

Pam nodded. "I'm going to an antique show in Billings
this weekend with my roommate. I've started a railroad
memorabilia collection. You know, serving dishes from the

dining cars, old timetables, things like that with the old Great Northern Railroad emblem on them.''

Pam changed collections more often than some people changed socks. It was hard for her friends to keep track of her collection du jour. ''Why don't you come with us?''

''Thanks, but I've got some reports to write. Maybe next time. It sounds fun.''

''Should be. Got a date tonight?''

''Nope.'' Terra's self-deprecating laugh revealed how little it mattered that she'd be spending the weekend alone. Most of the dates she'd had in the past year had been set up by Pam, with sometimes disastrous results.

Her heart wasn't in it. She believed in chemistry, and nobody she'd met yet had set off bells and whistles for her.

Pam realized she'd never met anyone more self-sufficient. Terra seemed completely content with her own company. ''Tomorrow night?''

''Nope.''

''I can fix you up with Buck Lincoln's brother.''

Terra flinched. ''Forget it. That last guy you fixed me up with was so empty-headed, I could've measured his IQ with a tire gauge. The one before that bellowed like a goat at the movie we went to. Oh,'' Terra reminded her friend, ''and don't forget you were the impetus behind my date with Poxie McNickle.''

''I thought he'd make you laugh.''

''That huge cowboy hat, which I might add he refused to take off all evening, was so big I felt like we were sitting under a patio umbrella. Plus, he's not the most ambitious man I've ever met,'' Terra declared with incredible understatement. ''What kind of man's life ambition is to run a fireworks stand? Working one month a year isn't exactly a career.''

''He needs his winters off so he can ski,'' Pam defended him with a snorting laugh. ''And you know he spends most of the summer at Zuercher Lake working on his tan.''

''No more blind dates, thank you kindly.''

"You're too picky. You'll never find Mr. Perfect."

"Then I'll keep looking."

"So," Pam surmised, "you'll spend another exciting weekend poring over journals on migratory patterns of North American wildlife. Ah, Terra, you sure know how to live life in the fast lane."

Pam's droll observation amused her.

"It's pretty hard to think about romance when I spend my days knee-deep in snow and mud, smelling like a bull elk." Terra raised one sleeve to Pam's nose to prove her point. "Besides, I'm waiting for bells and whistles to ring. I won't settle for less when I meet Mr. Right. Maybe I should just put an ad in the personals. 'Wanted: Native American man who likes classical music, chocolate, and women covered with elk hair.' "

Pam was familiar with her friend's background: born on the Crow Indian reservation, Terra had been adopted at infancy by the Bartlett family. She knew Terra adored her adoptive parents; yet the young woman had never denied her Crow ancestry.

Nor could she. With shining black waist-length hair and lively ebony eyes that danced, Terra's exotic, natural beauty elicited attention wherever she went. That she chose to ignore her beauty was part of Terra's charm.

"Speaking of Native Americans . . ." Pam broached the subject carefully, keeping her eyes on the rutted mountain road. "Have you ever thought of finding out about your birth parents?"

Silence in the truck hung heavy, nearly suffocating.

"No." The single-syllable answer was firm, definitive.

Never known for her ability to let something drop, Pam pursued it. "Why not? Do you feel like you'd be disloyal to your adoptive family?"

Terra shook her head. Her voice softened as she spoke of Mason and Nancy Bartlett, the only parents she'd ever known.

"No. They've always been completely honest and supportive. When I was younger, they told me if I wanted to search for my birth parents, they'd help.''

''And . . . ?''

In the greenish light reflecting from the dashboard, Pam saw Terra's face harden. ''My birth parents didn't want me. I don't want them.''

Ouch, Pam thought. *I've struck a raw nerve.* The look on Terra's face told it all. The face that usually held a sparkly eyed smile now appeared to be carved from stone.

The truck bumped along the darkened road. Headlights bouncing across the rutted snow provided the only lighting on the mountain route. Until the truck reached the road's end and turned onto the highway, the singular sound inside was the defroster humming its warmth across the windshield.

''Hope you don't mind my asking,'' Pam ventured. Terra was one of the kindest people she knew; Pam only wanted her to be happy.

''It's okay.'' Terra's smile was sad, weary.

''Really?''

''Yeah, really.''

The Fish, Wildlife & Parks Office sat at the edge of the state government complex, its overhead lights haloed this evening by the frigid, rolling fog. A thermal air inversion, prevalent in this part of Montana in early January, captured the damp cold and held it low in the atmosphere, obliterating any view of the stars.

''Looks like we're not the only ones burning the midnight oil,'' Terra observed as they pulled into the parking lot. Four golden squares of light at the end of the building indicated staff still in residence. ''The lights are on in the conference room.''

''Probably Ted Easton. I think he expected some bigwigs in from Washington, D.C., today.''

''Great.'' Terra grunted. ''Just what we need, Federal

bureaucrats getting in our way.'' Every time the Feds visited, the paper load in the office seemed to double.

The women entered through the back door and went directly to their respective offices. Monday morning, Terra would report on today's collaring activities. Tonight, however, it was enough to drop off the truck keys and check messages on her e-mail and answering machine.

Pam poked her head in the door. ''I'm outta here. Have a wildly exciting weekend.''

''Thanks.'' Terra's grin was tired. ''I will.''

''Oh, sure you will.'' Pam laughed cynically and disappeared into the darkened hallway.

Terra propped a hip on the edge of her desk and listened while her answering machine churned out messages. . . .

The dry cleaning was ready to be picked up.

Mom and Dad said Phoenix was great, they were going golfing, they loved her.

Her library books were overdue.

Please call Andy Worlen if she wanted to meet him for dinner after work Friday night.

Too late, Terra thought without remorse. Andy was a nice guy. But she didn't want to go anywhere, do anything tonight. It had been an exhausting day.

After jotting down the messages, she tidied her desk and turned off the computer. The truck keys were relegated to their usual spot on the peg. She flicked the switch to darken her office.

A long, hot bath and an order-in pizza sounded like heaven. She couldn't wait to get home.

''Excuse me . . .'' Resonating in the quiet office, the voice was deep, rumbling.

The silhouette in the doorway blocked out much of the blue-toned fluorescent glow illuminating the hall. Terra snapped the light on, flooding the office with glare. Her eyes rebelled for a moment, adjusting to the brightness. She batted her eyes like a toad in a thunderstorm.

"Excuse me," the man repeated. "I'm looking for a fax machine. Ted Easton told me I'd find one in here."

Eyes like luminous obsidian stared at her from a deeply tanned, firm-jawed face. They had a slightly brooding, sensitive aspect that Terra found terribly appealing.

Blue-black hair caught in a glossy, straight ponytail hung down the man's back. His lean frame wore a superbly tailored suit with stylish comfort.

He looks like a poster boy for Armani suits, Terra realized. That he was the handsomest man she'd ever seen was undeniable. Only his rugged, weather-beaten skin prevented him from being male-model perfect. He'd never see thirty again, she surmised, but the faint lines crinkling from the corners of his eyes only added character to an already distinguished face.

"Right over here." Terra waved toward the workspace in the corner. Never was she more cognizant of her scuffed pacs and the streaks of dried mud on her uniform. Hair that had escaped her braid during the day had seemed unimportant; now she was all too aware of the wispy strands adding to her disheveled appearance.

"I'm not very good with these gadgets." A lopsided grin tugged at one tan cheek as he fumbled with a handful of papers and eyed the fax machine with bewilderment. The smile subtracted ten years from his face.

"Here. Let's see if I might be able to help."

Terra jotted the number down as he read it in his distinctive deep voice. She inserted the report into the fax machine. Punching the keypad, she stood back with satisfaction as the roller grabbed the first page and the fax began transmitting.

"Thanks. I'm lost without a secretary." He shrugged apologetically. "Although she sure wanted to come to Montana with me."

The faint, spicy-clean smell of his aftershave clashed with her own game-and-mud aroma. There was nothing pleasant, Terra realized at that point, about smelling like a musky, range-run elk. Except maybe to another elk, she thought dismally.

The man stepped forward and thrust out a hand.

"I'm Whitman Bull Chief."

"Terra Bartlett." She shook his hand, then sheepishly grinned and pulled hers back, dusting her palms together. "Whoops, better be careful or I'll get elk hair on your beautiful suit."

"No problem." His manner was relaxed, friendly. "If it doesn't bother the elk to wear it, it shouldn't bother me either," he joked.

"It's just that . . . well, I worked game today and I'm kind of a mess." Terra's voice held a hint of apology. *Kind of a mess?* she asked herself. *Terra, you look like something that exploded.*

"You must be the Game Management Officer Ted Easton told me about."

"Ted mentioned me?"

White, even teeth contrasting against his robust complexion flashed as he smiled again. He did have a megawatt smile, Terra had to admit.

"I'm a liaison officer with the Bureau of Indian Affairs in Washington, D.C.," he explained. "Ted and I are on the phone about once a week for one reason or another. When he found out I'm a Crow Indian, he mentioned he had a Game Management Officer who's a Crow woman. But I wasn't expecting a Bartlett. Is that your married name?"

To some other woman, or at least under some other set of circumstances, the question might have sounded contrived. There were one hundred and one pat phrases a man might use to determine whether or not a woman was married.

Not for a moment, however, did Terra think it was a come-on to see if she had a husband lurking in the background. She had spent her twenty-seven years living as an Indian in a white world. Experiencing someone's surprise at her name or ethnic appearance was nothing new.

"I'm not married. Bartlett is my adoptive parents' name," she acknowledged. She scraped one thumbnail against the other, a nervous habit she had never been able to break.

Dark eyes locked on dark eyes as the two people stood over the fax machine, its rolling paper bail lending the only sound to break the silence.

"Well . . . well, that's . . . okay." His words were almost apologetic, as though he'd embarrassed himself asking a personal question of a stranger. More than once, his sisters had ribbed him for being too curious, for always asking questions.

He pursed his lips and blew out his breath, relaxing. "Terra Bartlett. It's a pretty name."

Despite his polished look of sophistication, Terra relaxed. Somehow he had managed to make her feel perfectly at ease. Her guard fell.

A smile crept over her face as she countered with, "Whitman Bull Chief. It's a noble name."

"Bull Chief's an old Crow name. Generations back. And my mother loves poetry," he explained. "I'm only glad she wasn't reading Longfellow when I was born. She wants me to promise that when I get married and have kids, I'll name one Byron."

So he's not married. Surprising, Terra thought. This guy could obviously charm the spots off a fawn. *Not married.* Terra surprised herself even more by realizing how glad she was of that. And yet, why could it possibly matter? He was a total stranger. She'd probably never see him again.

The fax machine continued to devour sheets from the report, churning them through slowly, page by page.

"Well, you were on your way out," Whitman continued. "I mustn't keep you. You've probably put in a long day."

His glance stole over her clothing. She certainly wasn't like the plastic princesses he'd met—some he'd even dated—who were constantly primping and vain.

No, she wasn't like that at all. He'd never seen so much

dried mud on one woman in his life. Still, she looked some-how natural. Unaffected. Beautiful.

Beautiful?

Yeah, he realized. *Beautiful.*

"We radio-collared elk up on Hannon Pass today." Terra's voice, although tired, couldn't hide the excitement of the day's project. She loved working in the field; being stuck in the office writing reports was not her forte.

"Interesting—"

"Exciting—"

Their concurrent comments elicited simultaneous laugh-ter. The air, nonetheless, seemed charged.

"That's something I've always wanted to see." Whit-man's voice held a note of wonder. "I've seen collared elk on the range but I've never witnessed the procedure itself."

"We'll be processing another herd in a couple of weeks," she offered. Why did she hold her breath, waiting for his response?

Settle down, girl, she warned herself. He was a total stranger. A gorgeous stranger with a heart-stopping smile. But a stranger nonetheless. And not even a local one at that. "I'm sure Ted would okay it if you wanted to ride along."

Regret saturated Whit's words. "I'll be going back to Washington tomorrow. But maybe the next time I'm in Montana . . ."

"Sure." Terra nodded. "That'd be great. Ted could make arrangements for you to ride up with me. Here—" She crossed to her desk and withdrew one of her business cards. Handing it to him, she smiled. "Terra Bartlett," she reminded him.

"Terra Bartlett," he repeated, his eyes reflecting her smile.

The fax machine spit out an activity report, signifying the transaction was completed. Sending its ending signal into the office, it whistled shrilly.

Neither person spoke.

"Well," Terra at last broke the silence. "I guess your fax is done."

"Thanks for your help, Terra."

His lazy grin was dynamite, Terra discovered.

She had eyes a man could drown in, he realized.

"You're welcome, Mr. Bull Chief."

"Whit."

Terra grinned. "You're welcome, Whit."

They shook hands.

Terra shook her hair back from her eyes and shut off the light after he left.

Whitman Bull Chief shook his head the next day as he drove to the airport, wondering why he couldn't stop thinking about the mud-splattered beauty in the FWP uniform.

Chapter Two

" "You've got to be kidding!" Terra's voice crackled with indignation.

" 'Fraid not." Max King tried unsuccessfully to keep a straight face. "You're it."

"What if I said I won't do it?" She hoped to call his bluff. But, Terra reasoned, he was her supervisor: she'd push it only so far.

"Ah, come on, Terra," Max cajoled. "Help me out here."

"What about Butch Reynolds? He was hired after I was. Doesn't seniority count?"

"Not in the realm of moosedom."

"Meaning?" Terra huffed.

"Meaning you're the only staff member skinny enough to fit into the moose costume. The high school student we hired to be Monty Moose didn't show up, and the children coming to the Winter Fair expect to see Monty Moose when they visit the Wildlife Building. It's traditional. We don't want to disappoint the little kids, do we?"

"We?" Terra emphasized, sarcasm dripping from her tongue.

". . . so just for this afternoon, I need you to be Monty Moose. Please?"

No, Terra reasoned. *I didn't get a master's degree in wildlife biology to dance around in a moose costume.*

No, this isn't in my job description. Besides, it wasn't politically correct, was it? A state employee masquerading

17

as a hoofed mammal? Wasn't there some kind of law against impersonating a moose? If not, there should be!

"Please?"

"Oh, all right," she acquiesced.

"You're a good sport," Max complimented. "I owe you for this."

"More than you can ever repay," she flipped back at him, not trying to hide her grin. Never in her life had she been asked to parade around as a moose. *Wait'll they hear about this at aerobics class,* she thought with a smirk.

The Fish, Wildlife & Parks Department building, a rustic log structure at the edge of the fairgrounds, housed educational displays and massive tanks of native fish. The displays brought fairgoers flocking to the building the first week in February each year during the Central Montana Winter Fair. Area grade-school children on field trips enthusiastically descended on Monty Moose at the FWP Building.

Max was right: Monty Moose was a tradition.

Tradition, scoffed Terra. She was all for traditions, as long as they didn't involve dressing up like a cartoon animal. It seemed less appealing by the minute.

She balanced on one foot, ramming the other into the leg of the brown plush moose costume. Positioning the rubber hoof over her shoe, she pulled the other leg on and squirmed into the suit. No, this wasn't going to be fun after all.

"If this isn't the stupidest . . ." she grumbled.

"Ah, she's a good-natured moose." Max's sides hurt from stifling his laughter.

"That's enough," she warned him. "You're going to pay for this, Max King."

"Back up over here," he instructed, "and I'll zip you in."

"I can't believe I'm doing this." Terra looked at her hands, now encased in rubber moose hooves. "This won't look professional on my résumé."

"Shut up and lean forward. Hold your braid up so I don't zip it in, or you'll be stuck in that costume forever."

Terra looked aghast. "What a thought!"

"Two hours. That's all I'm asking. Two hours as Monty Moose. Now"—Max looked around and found the rest of the costume—"now for the head."

Standing ramrod straight, Terra waited as Max positioned the moose head on her shoulders. The full-head mask reeked of garlic, a legacy left by the costume's last occupant.

Stretched over a wire frame, the cotton plush nose was padded with a layer of foam rubber. Where a wire had broken, it rubbed irritatingly on Terra's forehead. Life-size Styrofoam antlers forced her to drop her shoulders, compensating for the shift in balance.

Two hours inside this contraption? It'd be a lifetime, she was certain. If she didn't love this job so much, she'd resign on the spot.

"Don't let me hit the overhead lights with my antlers," she instructed Max. "I can barely see."

"Here. Let me move the tongue so you can at least see where you're walking." Adjusting the red felt tongue that flopped from the moose's mouth, Max cleared the vantage point from which the moose occupant looked out. The open mouth, covered at the back by mesh, afforded Terra a reasonably clear view of the exhibit building.

"It's hot in here," she complained. She had never realized before just how cathartic whining could be. "I think I have claustrophobia."

"Of course, Monty." Max raised his voice. "Of course you want to go see all the boys and girls."

Terra took the hint. It was showtime.

"I want a pencil," one child sniveled. "Where's my pencil, Monty Moose, where's my pencil?"

"I want a sticker!" another hollered.

"Monty! Monty!" A voice seemingly pitched decibels

above a dog whistle squealed constantly. Every kid in the place vied for Monty Moose's undivided attention.

And I thought this wouldn't be fun, Terra fumed from within the bowels of the hot, scratchy costume. *I'll get even with Max King if it's the last thing I do.*

"Hi, Monty Moose!" chirped a tiny boy, tipping his milkshake down her leg. One sticky hand waved. Monty Moose waved back.

A young mother pushed her recalcitrant youngster forward.

"Go see Monty Moose," she instructed her little one.

The child's face clouded up. "No!" His screech echoed throughout the crowded exhibit building.

His mother pushed him forward again. "Sure you can. Go show Monty Moose your nice new cowboy boots."

In an instant, the child's foot shot out, catching Monty Moose squarely on the shin.

"Yow!" Terra felt the impact through her thickly clad leg. The kid packed a wallop.

Never had two hours crawled along more slowly. Each minute found Terra enduring beverage spills, a few more kicks, cotton-candy blotches in her fur, and near heatstroke. Despite the cold winter day outdoors, the body heat from the crowd inside the building kept things plenty warm. Inside the moose costume, she reckoned, it was at least one hundred degrees. Her uniform shirt and slacks clung to sweaty skin. Her hair was sopping wet, plastered to her head. Wearing the heavy costume was the equivalent of a two-hour, high-intensity aerobics workout, without the luxury of breathing fresh air.

"Well, kids . . ." At last Max's voice boomed on the building's PA system. "Monty Moose has to go back to the woods now, so let's all say good-bye to him."

"Good-bye, Monty!" A hundred little singsong voices bid farewell as Terra plodded through the crowd, swinging her antlers to avoid a collision. At last she reached the door of the supervisor's office at the far end of the exhibit building, and stepped inside. Max was right behind her.

"I'm roasting!" Monty Moose complained. "Get me out of here."

"Lean over so I can pull your head off," Max sagely advised Terra.

He tugged at her full-head mask. Unencumbered by the confining head piece, Terra gulped in fresh air. Her face, flushed from the exertion and heat of the heavy costume, was streaked with perspiration. Her eyebrows were plastered down with sweat, and her eyes smarted from the garlic fumes in the mask. She was certain she'd never worked so long, and so hard, in her life.

"Thanks, Terra. Guess you'd like to take off early from work to go home and shower."

"Hint, hint." She laughed. A trickle of sweat escaped from her hairline and rolled down beneath the collar of her uniform shirt. She knew she looked a sight.

"Hello, Max . . ."

The man in the doorway looked from Max King to the half-woman, half-moose creature standing next to him. Recognition, and something more, flashed in his eyes as Terra turned to face him.

"Whit! Great to see you!" Max closed the distance between himself and the visitor, shaking hands. "Ted said you'd be in Montana sometime this week."

A devilish sparkle beamed from dark eyes that had inexplicably invaded Terra's thoughts the past month. Those eyes now danced as they swept the length of her moose costume and back up to the damp tendrils of black hair framing her face.

Max hurried to make introductions.

"Terra, this is—"

"Terra and I have met." Whit's voice was low, smooth. Grooves etched at the corners of his mouth suggested a lurking smile. "How have you been, Terra?"

The arrogance of the man, Terra huffed silently, *assum-*

ing I'd remember someone I met once, just briefly. And,
Terra realized in an instant, *I was as big a mess then as I
am now.*

"Mr. Bull Chief, isn't it?" She was deliberately obtuse,
hoping to take him down a peg. Her glance raked over his
features with a look designed to put him in his place. As
if he'd stuck out in her mind! As if she hadn't met dozens
of gorgeous men who dressed like fashion models and had
a voice like silk thunder and eyes like molten obsidian.

His grin told her he saw right through her. "It is. Remember? Named after the poet?"

So he had remembered their conversation, too. She
blushed, wondering why he flustered her so.

Max King didn't know exactly why he felt like an in-
truder on this scene. Maybe it was the way the two people
stood there gawking at each as though they'd forgotten he
was even in the room.

"Well," he interrupted the static-charged silence, "what
brings you to Montana, Whit?"

"I've got some work at the reservation this week, so I
thought I'd drive over here to say hello. When I swung by
the Wildlife Office, they told me you were down here at
the fairgrounds."

He had driven over a hundred miles out of his way on
winter roads just to stop by and say hello? Bewilderment
washed over Max's face.

Terra began to squirm out of her costume. Working the
zipper down, she peeled the suit to her ankles and stepped
out. One foot caught as she attempted to step free from it.

She lurched forward.

And was caught by rock-hard arms.

"You'd better be a careful moose," she heard as she
looked up into Whit's laughing eyes. "If you break a leg,
we might have to shoot you."

She pulled away quickly, blushing, and concentrated on
straightening her uniform shirt. Her hands shook as she
rebuttoned its top button.

Max watched Whit Bull Chief watch Terra.

"Well, I just gave Terra the rest of the afternoon off. After spending two hours as Monty Moose for the kids today, I think she deserves some free time."

"I think"—Whit looked from Max to the woman in front of him—"she deserves to be pampered tonight." His eyes locked on hers. "May I take you to dinner?"

"Good idea," Max answered for her. "Terra hardly ever goes out on dates."

Too late, Max realized how that sounded. Terra's cauterizing glare flashed at him.

"What I mean is . . ." the wildlife supervisor stuttered.

"Max . . ." the woman beseeched him. "Never mind." Embarrassment infused her grin.

"How about it, Terra?" Whit's invitation hung between them. "Would you like to have dinner with me tonight?"

If she had one hundred reasons why she shouldn't go out with the man, Terra couldn't think of any now.

Her eyes met Whit's. The sense of a silent understanding, now shared, seared through Terra like a lightning bolt. It was crazy, she knew. Absolutely crazy. No, she shouldn't go out with him. Definitely not.

She was astonished when she heard herself say, "Sure. That would be nice."

Well, I'll be, Max King thought to himself. He'd heard her turn down dozens of dates in the three years she'd worked for him. Her weekends were usually spent with her nose in a book. His glance bounced back to Whit.

The grin Whit wore was, Max realized, as big as a wave on a milk bucket. Had Whit ever spoken more than five words to any female in the office? Max didn't think so. The guy was quiet, deep. Heck of a nice guy, Max always thought.

And Terra was as flustered as he'd ever seen her. The blush on her face climbed clear up into her ears.

Well, I'll be, Max thought again.

* * *

"What looks good to you?" Whit folded the menu closed and stared across the candlelit table.

My dining partner, Terra thought but didn't answer.

"The scampi with pine nuts sounds great," she responded. The restaurant's ambience intrigued her. She'd never been to the Mountain Crest Inn before; too expensive for her wallet, its elegance was unmatched by any other restaurant in the area. Locally crafted pottery was teamed with fine imported crystal to lend a unique western flair to the table. A fresh-flower centerpiece adorned their damask-covered table, with a glimmering ivory beeswax candle nestled among the velvety blossoms.

Outside the wall of windows, lights from the ski hill glittered in the blackness. Moguls left by skiers' turns were accentuated in the light-and-shadow pattern covering the slope.

"What a night!" Terra's remark was directed at the moon-silvered landscape.

"Beautiful scenery," Whit agreed. Terra didn't notice that his eyes weren't focused outdoors.

Conversation came easily to the two. Politics, both state and national, held them riveted as Terra took a stand and Whit countered it. Their differences intrigued them; their shared interests captivated them.

When their discussion turned to current events, each impressed the other with the range of knowledge they both possessed. Whit was easy to talk to. There was no game-playing or guessing what would come next. He was forthright and deliberate, she could see. It was as though they had been friends for years. There was so much to talk about, so much to hear.

The meal finished, Whit folded his napkin and sat back. "You look lovely." His comment was quiet, matter-of-fact.

"Thank you. But you don't like this better than my muddy uniform, do you? Or heaven forbid, better than my moose costume?" She dropped her jaw in mock disbelief, trying to keep the moment light. He wasn't like any other date she'd ever known. There was a powerful intensity about him.

Half of her felt she'd known him forever; the other half feared she would never know him any better than she did right now. And that mattered.

And it terrified her that it mattered.

Whit's smile crinkled the skin around his eyes as he leaned forward, as if to intensify his scrutiny of her.

"Well, you looked okay that way, too. Like you're not afraid of real work. But I think you look extra nice in that dress."

"Thanks. I'm having a really good time, Whit." Her response pleased him.

"Me, too." He sat back in his chair and assessed the situation. A beautiful date, a four-star restaurant, being back home in Montana. *Ah, life is good,* Whit thought.

"Tell me about yourself," Terra prompted.

"Well—" Whit thought just a moment. "I like big dogs. Leather-bound books. I don't like cats in the house. I like pumpkin pie for breakfast. Don't like progressive jazz or paper cuts. I prefer multicolored Christmas lights to clear ones. I don't like operas sung in English. I'm partial to cold morning runs and red licorice. I still have my tonsils and my car is paid for."

"Seriously," his dinner companion insisted.

Whit's enumeration was brief, humble. "Graduated in Public Administration six years ago, worked for the Crow tribe, then transferred to the Bureau of Indian Affairs in Washington, D.C., three years ago."

"You like living in the capital?"

"It's not Montana, but it's not bad. Just different. It's interesting and exciting. How about you? Tell me something about yourself. Have you always lived here?"

"Went to MSU, worked summers in a music store, then on to graduate school. Started working for the Fish, Wildlife & Parks Service after that."

"Why the FWP?"

"Love of animals," Terra answered simply. "And I love the outdoors. I figured this was one way to combine my interests and get paid for it."

"You're good at your job. Ted Easton told me he wished he had ten employees as dependable as you are."

"I'm flattered." Terra blushed. "Our parents taught my brother and me that any job worth doing, is worth doing well. It sounds kind of hokey, I know, like something that should be written on a pillow cover or stuck on a bumper sticker, but it's true. I take pride in my job."

"Tell me about your family," Whit prompted.

"Dad's retired. He taught history at the high school. Now he's pretty involved with the Special Olympics program. He likes to read. I guess that's where I get it. Mom was a loan officer at the bank and retired last year. They snowmobile in the winter; in the summer they golf and garden. Mom's on the historical preservation committee, so she spends a lot of time poking around old buildings in the state with the thought of preserving them. My brother Willy is an attorney in New Orleans. He and his wife are expecting their first child soon."

"So you'll be Aunt Terra."

"Much to my pleasure."

"Would I be too nosy to ask"—Whit tipped his head to study his dinner companion—"why a gorgeous creature like you has never been married?"

"Of course you're too nosy." Coyness tempered her words. Her grin faded into seriousness. "I watched some of my friends get married in college; some even married right out of high school. It scared me when their divorces started being announced. I just wanted to make sure I marry for keeps. I'd take my time before deciding on something that important. It's a forever thing."

Having blurted out her feelings, Terra cringed. *Sure, Ms. Bartlett,* she thought grudgingly, *scare him off after the first date by talking about your ideas on marriage.* Her thumbnails clicked together nervously. She hastened to change the subject.

"What sort of work will you be doing while you're in Montana?"

"I have a meeting with the Northern Cheyenne on their health care facilities. We're still trying to recruit doctors to that area. At the Blackfeet Reservation, I have to talk to them about some business ventures they're exploring. Then I'll be visiting with the Crow tribal leaders with regards to mining rights on the reservation."

She nodded, but didn't respond. Whit wondered why.

"You've been to the Crow Reservation, of course?" He couldn't know it was like dashing ice water on her.

"No."

"Never?"

Terra shivered as she shook her head. "Never."

"But your people are Crow."

"My birth parents are Crow," she corrected him quietly.

"I have to be there in the morning for a meeting, but I could bring you back here tomorrow night. Come with me?"

"Thank you. No."

"Mind if I ask why?" He was interested in this woman. Whit couldn't deny it. It was more than her good looks. It was her brains, her independence, her spunk. She had that indefinable quality known as class, Whit recognized.

She swallowed to ease the tightness in her throat. "Maybe I need to explain something to you, Whit. I have never met my birth parents, nor do I want to. So when you ask about the reservation, no, I haven't gone there. I simply have no reason to go."

As an Indian, he had seen prejudice from white people. Sadly, he also knew Indians who had strong feelings against white people. The senseless distrust and intolerance on either side, Whit believed, was sad and misguided. But never had he expected to see a Crow woman whose resentment of her own people prevented her from discovering her heritage.

This is insane, he wanted to tell her. *This is stupid. You have every reason. These are your people.*

But this was also her choice. He wasn't involved. She was just a dinner date. A beautiful, intriguing dinner date. Nothing more.

Then why, he wondered, couldn't he shake the feeling that she would become something more in his life? Because he inexplicably felt himself wanting her to? It was more than simple attraction. Whatever it was, he'd never felt it before.

"A Crow always comes home." Whit's response echoed in her head long after he had left her at her front door.

Two days later, when Whit returned from the reservation, Terra found it easy to put wildlife surveys on the back burner and join him for lunch. Upon her return to work, the afternoon dragged as she entered data in the computer; she would rather be outdoors. Not even to herself would she admit it: she'd rather be with Whit.

With a promise of dinner at her condo and a quiet evening watching videos, Whit showed up at seven. They talked until after midnight, neither remembering afterward what movie they'd watched.

She learned he excelled at Scrabble.

He noticed the odd little habit she had of clicking her thumbnails together when she was concentrating hard.

She hoped he would stay for another cup of coffee.

He wondered if he would ever again feel anything as magical as he was beginning to feel for this woman.

The night before he left for Washington, he again took her to dinner. Conversation flowed as smoothly as the exotic coffee they shared over dessert.

"I should get you home." He glanced at his watch.

"We're working on mule deer studies in the office tomorrow," she conceded. "But I can get away to take you to the airport."

"I'll call you tonight," Whit promised. His voice was low, intimate, and Terra strained to hear it above the noise of the crowded airport.

"That'd be great."

"Could I have a kiss before I go?" The lighthearted question he posed conflicted with the feelings for her that weighed clear down to his stomach.

Her smile was all the answer he needed.

An encircling arm brought her against him. The warm pressure of his mouth covered her lips. It was a tentative kiss, exploratory and fleeting. Agitation knotted her stomach, struggling against the excitement that charged her nerves.

She smiled up at him, telling him wordlessly that she enjoyed being with him, appreciated her time with him. Relaxing naturally against his chest, she relished being cradled in his hold. The starched crispness of his shirt and the brocaded texture of his tie grazed her cheek as she hugged him tightly, then released him.

Their days together were over. Terra watched as he collected his briefcase from the scanning belt and turned to wave good-bye. His eyes held hers a moment longer, then he disappeared into the jetway.

The eastbound flight rolled to the far end of the runway, then nosed up into its angle of attack, climbing above the snowcapped mountains.

Terra watched it until the legendary blue of the Big Sky Country swallowed the plane as if it had never existed.

How, she wondered, could someone she'd known such a short time, leave such a void in her world?

"Sis?"

The phone had been ringing as she unlocked the front door of her condo.

"Willy! How's New Orleans's brightest new attorney?"

"Surviving. Have you heard from the folks?"

Hearing her brother's voice rocked Terra with a loneliness she found unfathomable. She was instantly transported to age six, showing Willy how to tie the laces on his sneakers, guiding his chubby little fingers to make a bow. Teaching him to whistle. Enlightening him about ghosts and rocket ships and bugs. Being his best friend.

No one could make her laugh like Willy did. No one could make things seem clear or right or hopeful like her brother could. Best buddies they'd always be.

"They're still in Phoenix. With the ten inches of snow we got last night, they'll probably stay down there another month or so."

"I tried you last night. Where were you?"

His sister's keeper, Terra mused.

"Out on a dinner date."

"No kidding?" William Mason Bartlett was astounded. His sister was dating? She found something more interesting on Friday night than migratory patterns of mule deer? Funny, it didn't sound like the Terra he knew.

"No kidding. How's Jennifer?"

"Beautiful. And big. The doctor even suggested the possibility of twins. We're due in less than six weeks."

Married the day after law school graduation, Willy had last year accepted a position with an established law firm in New Orleans. Now he was beginning a family of his own.

"Wills, you're so lucky."

"Don't I know it! Maybe we'll be like Mom and Dad, and have two kids in ten months!"

"Can you imagine them," Terra said with a laugh, "after nine years of marriage, adopting a month-old baby girl, then ending up expecting another baby!" Nancy and Mason Bartlett had done just that. Terra and Willy were eleven months apart in age.

Willy's enthusiasm was contagious. Jennifer was the

love of his life; the excitement of his impending fatherhood was the frosting on his cake.

"No wonder Mom's gray-haired," Willy's voice bubbled. "We were a handful. But she never lost her temper with us, did she? I hope if we have a girl, she has Mom's beautiful disposition."

The remark, cast out as smoothly and innocuously as a fishing fly, struck home.

It hit Terra like a punch: someday when she had children, she wouldn't be able to credit an ancestor with their eye color or their disposition or their quirky little habits. Or their medical history. What if, she panicked, she would pass on some unknown allergy or medical condition to her children?

"... like the fun we had when we were kids," Willy was saying.

Terra's mind came back to Willy's conversation on the other end of the phone line.

They both reverted to happy ten-year-olds during these weekly calls. A special friendship bonded Terra and her brother. They could talk about anything.

At length, Terra's demeanor turned serious.

"Wills," she chose her words carefully, "if a person wanted to look up something about his adoptive parents, where would he look?"

"She could look," Willy deliberately adjusted the gender in the hypothetical situation, "at the courthouse in the county where she was born. If the records on the adoption were sealed, she could call a good attorney, for instance her brother, and go from there. Each state's laws are a little different in terms of adoption, so the particular state in question would have to be queried."

"Not that I'm interested," Terra clarified.

"Not at all," Willy agreed. He had broken enough green horses in his day to know that reining them in too hard, too fast, didn't work. You had to slowly plant it in their head that it was their idea. Then you reined them in the direction you wanted to take them.

Chapter Three

Winds the last week in March, laden with pelting icy rain, swayed the trees alongside the highway. Every gust pulled at the truck, rocking it from side to side. Terra clenched the steering wheel with white knuckles.

"Springtime in the Rockies, ha!" she croaked sarcastically. "If this wind keeps up, my flight won't take off. Or if it does take off, we may overshoot Minneapolis completely and I'll get blown to New Jersey."

Max King glanced across the truck seat at the smartly dressed young woman behind the wheel. In her powder-blue short skirt and blazer, Terra looked more like a college beauty queen bound for spring break than a Game Management Officer assigned to address a national conference in Washington, D.C.

"It'll be all right," he assured her. How much of her concern, he wondered, was over her flight and how much was the anticipation of seeing Whit again?

He knew the two young people had kept the phone lines humming since Whit's trip out West last month. At first Terra had mentioned Whit's calls just casually. It wasn't long, however, until Max realized how much those calls meant.

She wanted to talk about them, about Whit, and the smile on her face when she mentioned him revealed more than she told. It was an ideal match, in Max's estimation. Whit Bull Chief was a heck of a nice guy, and Terra was a great gal. Yes, it was an ideal match.

As the plane leveled off at cruising altitude, Terra nestled into her seat by the window. The wind-bruised plains of North Dakota, barren and brown, flashed beneath her. After a brief stop in Minneapolis, the flight continued to Washington's National Airport.

Upon final approach, Terra reset her wristwatch two hours ahead and smoothed her sleek chignon. A touch of lip gloss completed her grooming. She breathed deeply and let out a ragged sigh of anticipation. Caught halfway between trepidation and excitement, she knew what was stirring her up inside. It seemed like a year since she'd seen the man who was on her mind day and night. Now, in a matter of minutes, she'd be with him.

He was waiting for her, as he promised he would be.

His face was tanned and stoic. His eyes scanned the crowd anxiously. He was totally unaware of the female attention he was attracting. More than one woman departing the plane cast an admiring glance at the tall, black-haired man as they passed him; his concentration, however, could not be diverted from the jetway door.

When he spotted her, his face broke into a broad grin that electrified his eyes.

She's beautiful, he thought. *And she's here.*

He stepped forward and took her arm, looking down at the face that had preoccupied his thoughts since he left Montana.

"Welcome to D.C." His eyes devoured her. "How was your flight?"

"Great!" She forced herself to marshal lighthearted friendliness, when deep within her, what she felt was quite something more. "And it'll be so good to see green grass. March definitely came in like a lion in Montana and it's been roaring ever since."

After retrieving Terra's luggage from the carousel, Whit brought the car around and loaded her bags inside. Her accommodations at the landmark Willard Hotel had been arranged by the company sponsoring her attendance at the conference.

"Your choice," Whit offered. "I'll take you sight-seeing now, or I can leave you to relax and unpack, then come back for you at dinnertime. I've got the whole day away from the office, so we can do whatever you like. Or, we can tour after your meetings tomorrow if you'd rather."

Not for a moment did she want that handsome face out of her sight. Not for a moment, either, did she want to admit to herself just how much it meant to her, seeing him again.

"I should review my notes for my speech tomorrow," Terra admitted, "but I'm too excited to concentrate anyway. Could we maybe go for a walk around the Tidal Basin?"

Whit nodded. "The cherry blossoms are just coming out. It'll be perfect."

They walked. And talked.

"Before I came to Washington the first time," Terra admitted, "I expected nothing but acres of gray government buildings. I never imagined all these beautiful parks."

Whit nodded. "It's an energetic, exciting place to be. There's always so much going on. But you don't want to be here during the Presidential Inauguration. Limousine gridlock makes the streets nearly impassable for about four days. Even on a daily basis, every time the President leaves the White House, it pretty much locks up traffic."

"I can't imagine it." Terra pushed an errant strand of hair back. "Some mornings when I drive to the mountains, I don't see another vehicle for miles."

"I know." Whit smiled, remembering. "When I worked on the reservation, I'd head down the highway and seldom see another car."

"Were you raised on the reservation?"

"From birth." The pride in Whit's voice was apparent. "Growing up in Blue Rock was heaven on earth. In the summer, my dog and I would hike through the hills. Swim in the creek. Hunt for rabbits, birds. I felt sorry for every kid who wasn't a Crow. It was an idyllic existence.''

"All your family lives in Blue Rock?''

"Two sisters there,'' he corrected her. "My eldest sister is a telephone lineman in Billings.''

"Interesting profession for a woman,'' she remarked.

"Yep. Kind of like being a game management officer,'' he returned with a grin.

They stopped under a full-limbed tree heavy with cherry blossoms. Sitting close to him on the park bench, Terra felt the comfort of his arm across the back of the wooden slats. It felt good, being so near him. He was comfortable to be with.

Late-afternoon sun, golden and warm, filtered through the leaves and danced mottled shadows across Whit's face as he smiled and turned to face Terra.

"Okay, I've told you about growing up Indian. Now you tell me about growing up in a white world. Did you like it?''

"It's all I knew,'' Terra explained. "Until I started school, I never really gave much thought to being Indian. My brother, Willy, and I had a wonderful childhood. We were raised in a household with an abundance of love and support. Our parents are great.''

"That's nice to hear,'' Whit interjected.

Terra nodded in affirmation. "I never thought of myself as different from anybody else in the neighborhood. My skin was a little different color from theirs in the winter, but in the summer we all looked about the same. I guess I never really thought about being Indian until I started school. In grade school, once in a while I overheard remarks. You know, sometimes children can be merciless to anyone different.''

"Not just children,'' Whit amended. "They learn intolerance somewhere.''

"Right. We had a schoolyard bully who delighted in grabbing another kid's wrist and twisting it both ways. He called it an Indian sunburn. Some of my classmates decided my ancestors invented it. Or they'd ask me where my feathers or my moccasins were. I remember being asked if I'd ever scalped anybody.''

"Have you?'' His eyes sparkled. She was fun to tease.

"You're disgusting.''

"You're beautiful.''

"You're excused.'' She laughed as he caught her hand in his, lacing his fingers through hers.

"May I take you to lunch tomorrow?'' He leaned forward, his appeal coming from his eyes before being formed on his lips.

Terra mentally reviewed her schedule. Meetings most of the day, a banquet afterward. It would be late before she returned to her hotel.

"Sorry.'' She meant it. "The day's pretty well planned.''

"Wednesday?''

"Meetings until noon, and then my plane leaves at three-thirty.'' Terra knew she'd be cutting it short just to get everything wrapped up before she was due at the airport.

"Then give me tonight?'' he cajoled. "Dinner, dancing, and I promise I'll have you back at your hotel at a reasonable hour.''

Georgetown had always been Terra's favorite place to shop when she visited the nation's capital. Now, at Whit's side, she discovered the fun spots for after-dinner entertainment. The pounding beat of music poured onto the street as they descended the stairway to one of the popular clubs below street level.

It was crowded on the darkened dance floor. Changing from a frenetic tempo to a soulful ballad, the music throbbed like a heartbeat. Slow. Steady. Rhythmic.

She had never before danced in Whit's arms. It was a heady, wondrous feeling. Her head rested against his muscular shoulder, relishing his closeness. Her hand was cupped in his. When she raised her face to his, he smiled and squeezed her fingers gently, silently reaffirming the joy he felt being with her.

Her senses were alive with the feel of him. His breath fanned against her cheek. There was a labored edge to his breathing. She could detect, at the base of his throat, the slightly uneven tempo of his heartbeat.

They swayed hypnotically to the song. The crowded dance floor seemed to disappear, leaving them alone, together. Vague impressions of light swirls and riveting music danced in and out of Terra's mind as she continued to move with Whit to the rhythm.

Others on the dance floor couldn't help but notice the attractive, exotic-looking couple so oblivious to their surroundings. That they were two people on the brink of falling in love was apparent to everyone except the two of them.

"Let's bring in the midnight hour by upping the tempo," the DJ announced as the volume and beat of the music were cranked up.

"Midnight?" Terra pulled her arm from around Whit's neck and confirmed the time with a glance at her watch. "I really need to get back to the hotel, Whit."

"Will you turn into a pumpkin, Cinderella?" he murmured, his lips against her hair as he continued to hold her close to him on the dance floor.

"Worse." She laughed. "I'll turn into a bore when I'm trying to give my speech tomorrow!"

"You really want to go?" An unspoken appeal shone in his eyes.

No, Terra thought. *I really want to stay in your arms and look up at your smile.*

No, I like standing at heaven's door.

No, I've never felt like this and I want it to go on and on.

"Yes, I really have to," she answered, affecting a lightness she did not feel.

They made their way through the crowd to the cool evening air outside. The streets of Georgetown were filled with the carnival-like revelry of college students, tourists, and partying locals.

In the mist-haloed lights of Foggy Bottom, the night was romantically subdued. Was this cloud-canopied sky holding the same moon she watched from her bedroom window in Montana? Perhaps. But here, tonight, it seemed magically transformed. It was softer, warmer. It was a moon, she realized, for falling in love.

The Willard lobby was quiet, sedately dignified, as Whit walked her to the elevator.

"I'll see you to your room." His voice was hushed, intimate. His arm stayed around her waist as the doors of the elevator yawned open. At her room, he took the key from her and unlocked the door. His lips brushed hers lightly, tentatively, as she opened the door and took the key from his warm hand.

"It's been . . ." She searched for a word to adequately describe being with him again.

Fun? More than that.

Wonderful? At least.

The best? Yes, and more so if she hadn't had to say good night to him now.

". . . wonderful," she finished. "Thanks for a great time."

After he said good night and walked silently down the thickly carpeted hallway, Terra leaned against the door of her room and tried to control her shaking knees.

There's no future in a long-distance romance, she cautioned herself. Besides, one simple good-night kiss shouldn't affect her this way.

But it had, she admitted. Like nothing she'd ever felt before, it had.

The conference room was crowded. Those attending the morning session stayed on for the afternoon meeting in anticipation of hearing the game officer from Montana address the grizzly bear issue.

As lights dimmed, Terra clicked the slide tray into focus and turned on the projector. She began by offering a brief history of the powerful grizzly bear population in the northwestern United States. Slides followed of specimens from cubs to fully grown grizzlies.

"Their distinctive silver-tipped fur and the hump near their shoulders are identifiable characteristics distinguishing them from the common brown bear," she explained to the eager crowd.

Flashing on the screen was a subdivided mountainside, testament to the extent of road building in the grizzlies' former habitat area.

"Last year's grizzly study," Terra announced, "confirmed thirteen known mortalities among the Crystal Mountain grizzly population. Two deaths resulted from management actions, four from illegal kills, two from train kills, one from lightning, three from natural causes, and one from an unknown cause.

"Land management agreements with private and corporate landowners and with the public will facilitate grizzly movement between the two management areas in question, and will help reduce human pressure on the grizzlies during the critical spring feeding period."

This was Terra's forum; her expertise in the area of game management was nationally recognized. Her presentation brought thunderous applause. She had held the crowd's interest the entire morning as few speakers could.

Meeting with Federal officials later, she was impressed with their interest in the grizzly bear recovery program. Their questions proved they had researched the grizzly–land developer issue.

Successive meetings throughout the afternoon were interesting and informative. Terra was in her element, explaining wildlife patterns and answering questions on migratory trends. Focusing on wildlife issues around the United States, the symposium was comprised of experts in their respective fields. As the Rocky Mountain States' only

representative, Terra's talks encompassed not only the grizzly bear recovery program but wolf reintroduction and
game bird habitat enhancement as well.

It was midnight when she returned to her hotel, her briefcase brimming with notes and reports she had collected
throughout the afternoon and early-evening sessions. She
fell into bed, exhausted, neglecting to check her messages
on the hotel's voice-mail system.

The next morning, her last in Washington, D.C., she was
in a hurry to get dressed for the half-day session, pack for
the airport, and meet her seminar colleagues for breakfast.

As she flew out of her room ten minutes late, the blinking
light on the phone signaled incoming messages. She
propped the door open with her briefcase and hurried back
to check the voice-mail messages.

"A message was received at ten twenty-nine p.m.," the
computer-generated voice droned.

Then Whit's voice, taped late the night before, cut on.

"Hi, beautiful. I'll be at the hotel at one-thirty tomorrow
afternoon to take you to the airport. See you then."

Terra paced between the registration desk and the staid
overstuffed sofa in the hotel lobby. It was one-thirty. Where
was he?

Minutes went by.

She checked her watch one more time, then compared it
to the clock behind the hotel desk.

Where was he?

If she wasn't at the airport soon, she'd miss her flight.

Three taxicabs pulled up to the front of the hotel and
departed with guests.

Still she waited. Where was he?

Finally, she hailed a cab and climbed into the backseat,
exasperated, as her luggage was loaded.

The cab pulled away from the impressive, historic structure, and turned onto Pennsylvania Avenue, merging into
the steady stream of traffic leaving the heart of the capital.

Several blocks away, Whitman Bull Chief sat in his car.

Seething with frustration and cursing the dead battery in his cell phone, he waited for the presidential motorcade to clear the intersection so he could get to the Willard Hotel before it was too late. With a flurry of sirens and flashing lights, the jumble of cars at last proceeded down the street, freeing traffic and reminding drivers of one drawback of commuting in the nation's capital.

Terra pulled her luggage from the trunk of Pam's car and rolled it up the sidewalk to her condo.

"Come in for a Coke? I brought you a snowglobe for your collection."

"Absolutely." Pam wanted to hear all about the trip. More specifically, she wanted to hear about Whit Bull Chief. Terra had mentioned nonchalantly—much too casually, in fact—that she'd be seeing Whit while she was in Washington. Pam's interest was piqued.

Terra hung her coat on the brass hook inside the door and kicked her shoes off. Padding across the oriental rug to the kitchen, she opened the fridge and pulled out two bottles. Pam followed and slid into one of the stools opposite the breakfast bar.

"You saw Whit." It wasn't a question. It was a statement of fact. The directness of Pam's remark amused her friend.

"I did."

"And?"

"And we went sight-seeing. He took me to dinner. We went dancing in Georgetown." Remembering the pleasure of Whit's company painted Terra's smile with wistfulness.

"How do you feel about him?" Pam slammed into the question with all the subtlety of a snowplow.

"We had a nice time." She was afraid to describe it with the depth she was feeling. It scared her, wanting so much to be with this man.

Pam blew out with exasperation. "A nice time? *Nice?* I can have a nice time at the Bagel Barn, stuffing down pesto-

and-onion bagels with veggie spread. This man is successful, he's intelligent, he's definitely interested in you. Not to mention that he's drop-dead gorgeous. You've just spent time with him dining and dancing in a fun spot like Georgetown, and the best way you can describe it is a nice time?''

"It was great," Terra upgraded her impression. "He's great.''

"But . . . ?''

"Well," Terra admitted, "I thought things were pretty good . . . uh, great. But he didn't take me to the airport.''

"That's why taxis were invented.''

"But he left me a voice-mail message at the hotel that he'd be there this afternoon to take me to the airport. He never showed up.''

"Something came up. I'll bet you that's it. He's a busy man. Something came up." She didn't know Whitman Bull Chief well, but Pam found herself making excuses for him. He didn't seem like the kind of guy who played games.

Terra shrugged, doubting herself more as she answered. "He has a cell phone. Why didn't he call?''

"He'll call you." Pam was certain. "There was a reason he didn't show up. He'll call you.''

"Maybe not. He's pretty sophisticated, Pam. Mr. East Coast meets Ms. Small-town Montana, you know. Maybe I bored him to death.''

"Baloney!" Pam was insistent. "He just works in D.C. He's a native son. Besides, he's definitely interested in you. Max King said Whit couldn't take his eyes off you at the fairgrounds.''

"Probably," Terra rationalized, "because he's never seen a grown woman dancing around like an idiot in a moose costume.''

"He's smitten.''

Terra's shrug dismissed the idea. "No more than I am," she answered honestly. "I can't get him off my mind. But nothing's going to come of it. For heaven's sake, Pam, the man lives three thousand miles away.''

"Well," Pam answered drolly, "it's not like you've got a boyfriend any closer."

"Thanks for pointing that out." Terra flicked at her friend's head with a kitchen towel.

"Only because you never wanted one until Whit came along," Pam reasoned.

Practicality drenched Terra's response. "But three thousand miles is too far to carry on a romance."

In the midnight darkness of her condo after Pam left, Terra realized the flaw in that reasoning. Whit may have worked thousands of miles away, but, she realized, he lived within her heart.

Somewhere outside Whit Bull Chief's condo complex, a car door slammed. Further down the street, a dog barked. In the distance, a siren wailed.

Whit flipped over in bed and crumpled his pillow under one arm. The alarm clock read a little after two. Sleep had eluded him since he came to bed.

It was midnight in Montana. She'd be asleep after her busy, long day. The flight itself would've taken most of her day. He couldn't call her now.

Yes, he could.

He had to.

He had to hear her voice.

"Terra?"

She had grabbed the phone on the first ring, knowing, hoping, praying, it would be Whit.

"I'm sorry I had to stop for a motorcade and my cell phone wasn't charged and when I got to the airport your flight was taxiing and I just wanted to see you again." His words rushed out in a stream. The anguish of missing her tightened his voice.

"It's okay." Her voice softened. "I understand."

"I just called . . ."

The line was silent.

"Whit?"

"Yeah. I, uh, just called . . . uh," he tried again.

"You called . . ." Terra prompted him.

"I, uh, called because I need to tell you something, Terra."

"Go ahead, Whit."

"I can't stop thinking about you, Terra. What would you say if I told you I'm falling in love with you?"

The sharp intake of her breath was audible over the phone line. She was speechless.

"Terra?"

"Yes?"

"Talk to me."

She swallowed and pushed her hair back. Clinging to the phone like a lifeline, she found her voice again.

"I don't know what to say, Whit, except that it's insane. We've known each other such a short time."

"I know, I know. But I'm new at this, Terra. I don't know how long it should take. I've had women in my life before—friends, dates—but nothing has ever smacked me between the eyes like this feeling I have for you. The first night I saw you, something just clicked. I've tried to work it out in my own mind, what's happened. I feel like I've been struck by lightning. I can't describe it to you."

"You don't have to, Whit . . ."

The phone line was brittle with unspoken energy.

". . . you don't have to describe your feelings to me," Terra continued. "I've felt the same way from the first time I saw you. It's crazy. It scares me to death. I'm trying to be sensible about it. There's no future in it. There's a little matter of several thousand miles between us, for starters."

"I can change that." Whit's voice held no hesitation. He'd been all through this in his own mind, already. "I can transfer back to Montana."

Terra attempted to quell the shiver of anticipation that crawled up her spine. "You've worked hard to get where you are, Whit. I can't ask you to do that for me."

"I wouldn't be doing it just for you. I'd do it for me.

I'm a native son, honey. Montana is where I'm happiest. Besides''—she heard Whit chuckle—''my thoughts and my heart've been in Montana with you anyway. I might just as well get the rest of my body out there, too.''

''Are you sure of this, Whit?''

''I don't know if I've ever been more sure of anything. I've been hashing this over in my mind since the minute I picked you up at the airport. I need to be around you, Terra. My head hasn't been on straight since I first met you. Something's been missing in my life, but I never knew it before. It's you, Terra. There's something about you that makes me feel complete. I'll start working on a transfer tomorrow, and if everything goes okay, within six months I can be back in Montana permanently.''

''It's a big step,'' Terra whispered as much to herself as to him.

''Too big for you?'' Whit had to know. Everything in his life would revolve around her answer.

''Not if you're here with me, Whit.''

It was the answer he wanted to hear.

Terra had barely stepped foot in her office the next morning when Max King called her in.

''Need you in my office pronto,'' he snapped. There was none of the usual humor she was accustomed to hearing in his voice.

They'd worked together long enough for Terra to recognize the tension in her supervisor's tone. It held that ominous near-growl that spelled trouble. When she entered his office, Max's expression startled her.

''What's happened, Max?''

''Sit down.'' He nodded toward the chair facing his desk, but his mind wasn't on office courtesies.

''I'll stand, thanks.'' He was making her nervous. ''Tell me what's wrong.''

''We just got a call from a couple of joggers who spotted

a collared wolf somebody shot and left on the river bank out by Mile Marker 326.''

A physical blow couldn't have hit her any harder. Terra reeled from Max's desk, overwhelmed by the horror, nearly to the point of nausea. She backed against the chair and folded into it.

"It's R-21, isn't it?" She referred to the animal by his red ear tag. For months, the radio collar on the huge gray male wolf had failed to transmit. Normally, the signal was a steady beep. If for some reason the collar was immobile, either having been lost or on a collared animal that died, the signal increased in frequency to what the department referred to as a mortality signal.

None had been received on this particular wolf. He had just disappeared from tracking. Several attempts to locate the wolf during aerial searches had been unsuccessful. Now, their worst fears surfaced.

"I'm afraid so." Max's face was pale. Words could not express his contempt for anyone who would destroy a beautiful animal without cause. The wolf was some distance from any ranch property; it hadn't been shot by a beef producer defending a herd.

"How long has he been dead?" Terra pushed her hurt deep inside, not allowing it to overshadow her professionalism. "We need to get him into the lab."

"We'll check all that when we get him back here. Pat Bohardt's loading the truck now. I want you to go with him. I'm sending Pam with Nate Barker, too. They're up by Ten Mile Creek now. They'll meet you at the spot."

Terra had been there the day the wolf was released from captivity. He was a huge, proud animal. She had never forgotten the look of intelligence in his molten gold eyes. Hundreds of miles from his release point, he had obviously relished his freedom until an unknown coward's bullet snatched that freedom in one horrible moment.

* * *

Gorged ice from the river lay along its banks, jutting up from the thawing ground like tombstones in a graveyard. The sky, overcast and gray, draped the afternoon in a dismal canopy of blackening clouds.

"Terra, I'm sorry," Pam said simply as they left their trucks. "I know you had a special interest in this one."

"I tracked him when he left captivity," Terra explained unnecessarily. "When his collar quit signaling, I hoped he had just rubbed it off somewhere and the battery died. But I guess in my heart, I was afraid something like this might have happened."

The majestic wolf, his body partially frozen in the ice at the water's edge, still retained his collar. A glance at the red ear tag confirmed his identity.

The four FWP staff members loaded the creature's body in the truck. Terra steeled herself to maintain her composure.

"We'll take him straight to the lab," Pat reported to the women. "They'll be waiting for us."

After walking the riverbank for more than an hour, they found nothing to help identify the culprit who had shot the wolf.

"Somehow, someday, I'm going to find out who killed him." The hurt in Terra's voice was replaced by cold determination.

She couldn't know at that moment how prophetic her words would prove to be.

Chapter Four

Springtime in Montana was heralded with a special sense of urgency, as though Mother Nature were in repentance for the long, hard winter.

Sprigs of green buffalo grass poked through the rapidly diminishing snow cover alongside the Missouri River. The waterway was swollen from the winter runoff. April's rains were on hiatus today; the blue sky was cloudless and vast.

Quaking aspen anticipated longer days of sunshine to burst their tight green buds into coin-sized silvery leaves that fluttered and danced with each breeze.

Collin Edwards hurried to keep step with Terra. She moved faster than anybody he'd ever seen, covering the distance from the road to the riverbank in long, purposeful strides.

"Will you slow down, for heaven's sake? You always walk like you're on fire." The falconer huffed, his long legs no match for her energetic pace.

Collin had worked with Terra for two years on the peregrine falcon recovery program. He enjoyed his association with the bright, attractive young woman. There was a time, Collin would admit only to himself, when he had hoped his affiliation with Terra would grow into something more than a working relationship. But she had never indicated anything more than a professional interest in the bespectacled, shy bachelor; he respected her enough to keep things on those terms.

Terra's face was flushed with excitement. Her ebony

eyes danced. "I can't wait to see Cheepy. It's been almost a month since I checked the hacking boxes with Pam."

"He'll probably be ready to hunt his own food within the next few days," Collin pointed out. The peregrine falcon, dubbed "Cheepy" by the FWP workers who were fascinated by the hatchling's vocal persistence, was part of an experimental release program using the "hacking" technique.

The screen-sided hack box housing the young falcon had been stationed in the woods near the Missouri River, where prey was plentiful.

Collin, as an experienced falconer and wildlife volunteer, had fed the bird regularly until its flight feathers matured. Today, they would remove the screens. Slowly, as the bird developed its ability to hunt, Collin would wean it from provided food. In time, the hacking box would be removed entirely as the young adult peregrine became self-sufficient.

As they entered the designated area, the sound of chirping racketed from the hacking box.

"He's calling for the chef," Terra teased.

"He'd better get used to hunting for himself," Collin reminded her. Reaching for the screens, he pulled them free from the frame.

They stepped back. Although Cheepy had grown somewhat accustomed to the sounds of humans, he was still a wild creature. Their movement was minimal; any sudden motion would startle the bird.

Mystified, the young falcon remained within the enclosure, his head cocked to one side.

"Go on, you," Collin spoke softly to the bird. "You're free to go."

The peregrine took tentative steps toward freedom, then ruffled its feathers and lifted from the ground in an awkward attempt at free flight.

"I'll be back a couple of times this week to put out food, but as he grows accustomed to hunting, I'll wean him. Before long, he'll relinquish his dependence on us as a food

supplier and be on his own.'' The pride in Collin's voice
was obvious. He'd worked in the recovery program long
enough to know the success rate. It was a worthwhile
program.

"I've recorded the date and time for our reports.'' Terra
glanced up from her field notebook and smiled. "Good job,
Collin.''

The tall, angular falconer shrugged bony shoulders and
waved off the compliment with one hand. "Glad to be of
help. Anytime.''

"I appreciate that.'' Terra knew if it weren't for dedicated volunteers, the raptor recovery programs in the northwestern United States would diminish.

She glanced at her watch. "Better be getting back to
town. It's nearly five.''

"You've never been a clock-watcher before, Miss Bartlett. What's come over you? Got a hot date?'' Collin was
kidding. Still, he almost hoped she would say no. Maybe
she'd go have pie and coffee with him after work.

Her blush told it all. There was a guy on her mind.

"Collin, I'll tell you what's come over me.'' They
walked toward her truck. The sun danced highlights across
the thick black braid bobbing down her back. She turned
toward Collin with a megawatt smile. "I've fallen in love.''

"No.'' He was dumbstruck. *Lucky dog, whoever he is,*
Collin thought.

"Yep. His name is Whit Bull Chief. He's with the BIA
in Washington, D.C. He's planning to transfer to Billings
in September if everything goes through all right. Which
is a good thing, because his phone bills must be astronom-
ical. He calls me every night.''

"Well.'' Collin held the truck door for her, then went
around and climbed in the passenger side. "Well, that's
just great.''

"It is, isn't it!'' The exuberance reserved only for those
in love surrounded Terra. "He's wonderful.''

"So you're probably going to be a married woman by the end of summer."

Terra concentrated on starting the truck's engine and steering along the muddy road.

"We haven't talked marriage . . . yet," she emphasized. "We need to spend some time together. Get to know each other, you know?"

Collin nodded.

"Then," she continued, "we'll go from there."

"Do you see marriage to him a possibility? Is that what you want?"

"Someday, yes." Terra's answer was more for herself than for her colleague. "Someday, definitely yes."

"Best wishes." Collin smiled and patted her shoulder. She was a heck of a woman. She'd make a dandy wife. *Whit Bull Chief, you're one lucky dog,* he grumbled to himself.

"One more week." Terra marked the day off her kitchen calendar with a pen. "Whit's coming for the Indian Pow-wow at the university. He'll be here next Friday."

"Is his family coming from the reservation, too?"

"Whit said they're not. His mom was washing windows a couple of weeks ago and backed down off the ladder crooked. She twisted her ankle and fell. She broke her leg and now it's in a cast. But Whit'll be going to see them after the Powwow. I wish," she reflected, "that I had a chance to meet his folks. But maybe they'll be in town this summer. In the meantime, I'm just anxious to see him. Just think—one more week and he'll be here."

Pam tipped her wooden stool onto its back legs and rocked contentedly. "One more week for you to practice this chocolate cake recipe." She jabbed her fork into the dessert and brought a heaping portion to her mouth.

"You like it?"

"Whoa!" Pam closed her eyes and sighed contentedly.

"You might just end up with domestic skills after all, girl! This cake is heavenly."

She smirked as Terra cut another slice and dumped it on her plate.

"Speaking of skills, how 'bout testing our canoe-paddling skills on the Madison this afternoon? Are you up to some river running?" Terra cocked her head to one side, challenging her friend.

The Madison River, relatively ice-free as a result of its thermal input from Yellowstone Park, was the first recreational waterway navigable each spring. A sure harbinger of winter's end was the canoe armada on the river the first sunny weekend in April.

With a rasping squawk, the aluminum canoe slipped atop the rack on Terra's pickup as both women pushed to position it. Pam threw the paddles and life jackets in the box of the truck.

"Spring has been a long time coming this year." Terra backed out of the condo's driveway and turned toward the highway. "It's good to see the days getting longer."

Newly sprigged cottonwoods waved hello on the gentle springtime breeze as they took the highway, crossing the line into Madison County.

Twenty minutes later, the women unloaded the canoe and threw their gear into the bottom of the boat. Lapping at the shore, the water was crystal clear. The smell of awakening earth carried on the breeze.

They pushed off, each adjusting their strokes to propel the vessel toward the middle of the river. The blue sky, gloriously bright and unclouded, met the river some distance ahead on the horizon. Cranes hung above the water like gossamer kites, dipping with the breeze then soaring toward the sun and swooping downward again.

"Heaven on earth!" Pam's exclamation mirrored Terra's thoughts.

"No place I'd rather be."

"No place? Ha!" Pam's cynical laughter rang across the river. "You'd rather be with Whit!"

Terra nodded. "By golly, you're right. I nearly forgot about him." Poignant memories of their times together drifted across her mind like ripples in the river.

"Oh, sure, sure," Pam mocked her with an exaggerated agreement. "I never thought I'd see you like this. Imagine my buddy, an old married woman."

"I'm not married yet," Terra reminded her.

Pam ignored her. "And then, the next thing we know, you'll be starting a family."

Terra paddled industriously.

" 'One little, two little, three little—' " Pam sang.

Terra's paddle left the water, scooping what Pam felt must be half of the Madison River with it, as she got doused.

"Oops, sorry, Pam. It slipped," Terra yelled in mock horror.

"Sure it did." Pam giggled as she wrung out her ponytail. "I mention having babies and immediately you get all excited. Better learn how to use that paddle. In more ways than one!"

"I'm not afraid of babies, for heaven's sake," Terra protested. "After all, Willy and Jennifer's twins are wonderful. When those two boys grow a little, Aunt Terra's going to teach them to canoe and play ball and . . ."

"And eat chocolate cake."

"Whatever they want," Terra agreed. She couldn't wait to see the babies in June when she'd be vacationing in New Orleans, visiting Wills and Jennifer.

The rhythmic glide of paddles in water lulled the women into a nearly hypnotic peace.

"Terra?"

"Yeah?"

"When you think about marrying Whit and starting a family of your own, aren't you just the least bit curious about your birth parents? They'd be your kids' grandparents.''

''No, they wouldn't. They'd be strangers, just like they are to me now.''

''Not if you found them and let them be part of your life.''

''Pam, you know how I feel about that whole thing. They gave me away.''

''But what,'' Pam persisted, ''if they had a good reason for giving you up?''

''What reason would be good enough for a mother to take her own baby and hand it over to a total stranger?'' The hurt in Terra's voice crackled, surfacing despite her attempts to remain indifferent to the matter. ''What possible reason?''

It was a question she'd asked herself hundreds of times. And how frustrating it was not to have an answer!

''Maybe the mother was sick. Or poor. Maybe she just couldn't afford to keep you. There are lots of legitimate reasons why a mother may have to sacrifice her own happiness by giving a child up for adoption.''

''Then again . . .'' The hurt in Terra's voice came through brittle and caustic. ''. . . maybe she had no good reason at all.''

''You'll never find the answer if you won't go looking for it.'' Pam's quiet remark hung in the air like smoke.

They drifted with the current now, the silence of the river broken only by the occasional cry of a gull.

''Hi, gorgeous.'' The voice on the phone was low, silky.
''Whit! Where are you?''

''I just landed in Billings. My sis is here to take me to her place tonight. I'll drive up tomorrow morning . . . leave here around seven. It shouldn't take me more than two hours to get there.''

The pounding in her knees rivalled the pounding in her heart. Her smile threatened to break her jaw.

She glanced at the clock. Four hours until midnight, then nine more until she'd see him. Every hour would be three days long until he got there.

The university field house was a glaze of multihued costumes as Indian tribes from all over the northwest gathered for the Grand Entry of the Powwow.

The tinkling of trim on dance costumes, coupled with the practice drumming, blended with voices to create a lively cacophony clear out to the parking lot.

Whit had stopped by Terra's condo briefly that afternoon on his way to the Powwow, extracting her promise she'd be along in time for the opening ceremony.

Now, she watched as the participants convened for their celebratory gathering. She was struck first by the gaiety of the celebration. It was a many-layered gathering: family reunion, barbecue, and dance contest. People stood in groups, renewing old friendships and introducing one another to new acquaintances. Booths offering beaded handiwork, leather wares, and quilts bordered the dance area. Children decked out in traditional Indian costumes wove in and out of the crowd, running off excess energy as they too renewed friendships since the last powwow.

Nancy Bartlett sat at her daughter's side, watching Terra as much as she was watching the festival itself.

"... We have a baby for you, Mrs. Bartlett. She's two weeks old. You and your husband can come get her next Thursday. She was born to a Crow Indian woman ..."

It seemed like only yesterday. Then today's call came, Terra asking Mason and Nancy to join her at the Powwow, to meet Whitman Bull Chief.

Willy had warned his parents: this was the guy. This was the man who had turned Terra's world upside down and put that special sparkle in her eyes. His close bond with his sister allowed him to understand her better than she understood herself sometimes. She was afraid of these blossoming feelings, he knew, but they were there just the same. Terra had fallen in love, whether she would admit it to her family or not. Every time Willy talked to her on the phone, he believed it more strongly. His sister was in love, for the first time in her life.

Mason had a meeting he couldn't bow out of, so he sent Nancy with firm instructions to learn all she could about their daughter's beau. Nobody would ever be good enough for his little girl, Mason steadfastly determined, but at least he'd give the young fellow a chance.

The arena was filling quickly. Bleachers provided the audience an overview of the festivities. It was a sea of dancers, singers, and visitors.

"We will now begin the Grand Entry. Everyone, please stand." The speaker's voice reverberated through the field house, echoing back to itself a split second later.

"I can't find Whit." Terra's brow wrinkled in concentration as her eyes scoured the field house.

Their attention was drawn to the double doors of the arena, which were now flung open. Filing in slowly, with great dignity, were Indian men in full ceremonial garb carrying a variety of flags. Old Glory was at the forefront. Behind it came the colorful flags which, a spectator behind Terra pointed out, were the various tribal flags. Wearing their ornate headdresses, some of the men looked larger than life, as though they'd stepped off a movie screen.

After that came the honored guests. The veterans, those modern-day equivalents of warriors, led the next group in the procession, followed by other important guests. Tribal chiefs, princesses, elders, and the Powwow organizers came next in line. Behind them, the men dancers entered, a study in grace and decorum. Finally, the women dancers completed the line.

As the procession circled the field house and halted, the flag was presented at center court. The Indian National Anthem, the Flag Song, blared from a sound-system tape recorder.

Earl White Bear, introduced to the crowd as having just

celebrated his one hundred and second birthday, offered a prayer. The hypnotically beautiful Crow language sang across the gathering as the old man prayed.

Upon its completion, the crowd roared its approval and the festivities began.

One theory said that the powwow was named for Algonquian spiritual leaders or medicine men. The phrase *pau wau* had been transferred by Europeans to refer to the entire event. From those medicine-men dances, the tradition had evolved into gatherings which included visiting, dancing, singing, and gambling.

"Some people confuse the powwow with religion," Whit had told her, "but it is a social activity, designed to maintain a connection to traditions. It's an intertribal activity. Indian nations are gathering under a flag of peace and are socializing together. We are celebrating being alive."

The focus tonight was the dancing. Open social dances, called intertribals, would mix with several categories of dance competitions.

Round dances sent buckskin-clad men twirling and executing their intricate steps with a precision honed from years of practice.

As quickly as it had begun, the dancing suddenly stopped. A man stepped forward on the speaker's stand, offered a prayer, and the dancers returned to the floor.

Nancy leaned forward. "What happened?" she asked an Indian seated beside her.

"An eagle feather fell from a dancer's headdress," the woman explained. "We consider the eagle sacred. When the feather falls to the floor, the dancing stops. We say a prayer before beginning to dance again."

The steady, rich sound of the drums beat a tempo that became indistinguishable, Terra realized, from her own heartbeat. Fascinated with the dancers, she broke her concentration only long enough to scan the group of men waiting to dance next. At the end of the arena, she spotted Whit.

He bore little resemblance to the man she had seen earlier in the day. Gone was the well-cut, expensive tailored clothing Whit wore with such flair. No crisp white shirt or tasteful silk tie was in evidence tonight.

His hair, gleaming blue-black under the huge field-house lights, hung in two braids caught at the ends with leather ties. His broad shoulders showed the beaded-yoke leather shirt to great advantage. Just short of appearing savage, his chiseled, stoic face was reminiscent of the great Indian chiefs Terra had read about in history books.

Surrounded by the dancers from his tribe, he stood a head taller than the other men. His skin was tanned a deeper bronze than when she had first met him this winter, matching the rich color of the men in his group. His eyes glowed like hard chunks of obsidian.

This wasn't the Whit who clowned around with her, biting the end off his ice cream cone and sticking it on his nose like Pinocchio.

It wasn't the gentle creature who kicked off his shoes and played Scrabble on the floor with her. Nor was it the man who jitterbugged to old-time rock and roll with her in the kitchen.

And it certainly wasn't the sentimental giant who stuck cherry blossoms in her hair and kissed her fingertips.

No, this man looked carved from granite.

Unyielding.

Unrelenting.

Formidable.

No one, Terra was certain, would want to trifle with Whitman Bull Chief. He exuded no softness tonight. This Whit would not be one whom anyone would want to cross.

She watched him nod at something being said in the group. His face was somber. The dance competition was serious business for all participants.

Then, magically, he gazed up into the bleachers and found Terra. His face transformed as he saw her, his bright smile mirroring her own.

Breaking away from his group, he walked with the lithe,

ambling gait Terra had come to love, to the bottom of the section of bleachers where she sat.

"Come down," he mouthed to her, over the din of the crowd, motioning to a clearing on the crowded floor.

So this is the man who has stolen our daughter's heart, Nancy appraised him. He was certainly handsome, and seemingly unaware of it. And, she noted as he was greeted by fellow dancers, extremely popular. Obviously, he enjoyed interaction with people.

A good sign, Nancy thought with approval.

"Go to him," Nancy insisted. "I'll meet him after the dancing."

She watched her daughter descend from the bleachers to meet the man in her life. Terra's body language told it all. Standing near Whit, her shoulder comfortably touching his arm, Terra's face grew animated as she visited with Whit's friends. But it was the look in her eyes when they settled on Whit, that told Terra's story.

The girl was clearly, completely in love.

The sound system crackled to life as the next round of dancing was announced. The clusters shifted; singers around the drum stepped back to allow the next group to perform.

The head man dancer, a visiting Sioux from North Dakota, stepped forward. His shirt, trousers, and apron bore the yarn fringe characteristic of the *Peji Waci,* or Grass Dance. After the lead line was sung first by the head singer and then by the second singer at the drums, everyone joined in.

The drum, the heartbeat of the Earth Mother, brought the people of the Powwow into balance. Whether dancing, singing, or just listening, the Indians glorified in the steady, pounding rhythm.

The Grass Dancer began. The tamping movements of moccasin-covered feet was reminiscent of Indians one hundred years before, stomping down the grass on the prairie in preparation for dancing. The dancer's loose, flowing sway continued, keeping beat with the resounding drums. His outfit, decorated traditionally with the hearts, clubs, spades, and diamonds of playing-card designs, flashed as he led the group of dancers in a circle. The custom of some tribes wearing braided grass in their belts to symbolize enemy scalps, was thought by some to have given the Grass Dance its name. Now, the dancers depicted fierce warriors as they wove in and out, circling the arena.

Dance judges strolled at the edge of the area, marking their clipboarded scorecards for each dancer. Some dancers, like rodeo riders, traveled the circuit to compete for top prize money. Others like himself, Whit had told her, did it for the tradition and for the enjoyment of getting together with his old friends.

"We're dancing next," Whit explained. His feet had already begun a soft percussion on the wooden floor of the field house. His Cheyenne-style rawhide-soled moccasins were beaded, a gift from his mother, he told Terra proudly. A bone hairpipe choker circled his sinewy neck.

"I'll be watching with Mom." Terra pointed up into the bleachers where Nancy watched the two intently.

Whit nodded and smiled in Nancy's direction, although he couldn't pick her out in the crowd.

"I'll see you," he promised Terra softly, "after the gourd dancing."

He wanted to kiss her. But it wasn't appropriate here, now, he realized. So he settled for squeezing her hand, relishing her touch.

The drum's beat vibrated in Terra's throat. Or was it her heart? she wondered. The hypnotic sound pulsated through the crowd, lending a surreal aura to the groups as they circled the drum. As if in a dream sequence, in a blur of feathers, fringe, and fans, they whirled. Some wore face paint. Whit's face, though free of adornment, held an expression of rapt concentration.

When the song ended, the master of ceremonies announced the gourd dance.

"This dance originated from the Kiowa tribe and is a religious form of dancing," he announced. "Our dancers are asking God to look down on the people who have gathered to celebrate."

Dancers entered the ring, carrying gourds decorated with feathers, string, beads, and horsehair. Rotating slowly, the dancers shook their gourds, and as the tempo changed to a louder, stronger beat, each dancer stopped and again shook the homemade instruments. Thunderous applause greeted the dancers as they filed from the floor.

"Whit's going to meet us at my condo," Terra informed her mother as the Powwow drew to a close. "He wants to shower and change clothes before he comes over."

Look at them, Terra thought as she watched her parents and Whit finish their apple pie and coffee. They laughed and talked as though they'd known one another for years. What was not to love in all of them? Terra smiled to herself. How lucky she was!

"Is this the man who'll give us grandchildren?" Mason's voice was quietly frank in the kitchen as he and his daughter loaded the dishwasher. In the front room, Nancy was again laughing with Whit.

"I hope so, Dad. I know I love him."

"He feels the same way. I see it in his eyes when he looks at you, talks about you."

"He's a good man, Dad. Just like you. Both of you have my heart."

"Have you talked about marriage?"

"Not yet. We've talked about spending more time together, getting to know each other better. This has happened so fast, Dad. I need to be really sure. Marriage is a lifetime commitment, like for you and Mom. The chemistry is definitely there, though. I knew he was special the first time I saw him. Nobody's ever affected me the way Whit does." She blurted it out, then blushed as she realized this was her dad she was talking to.

It was after midnight when the Bartletts bade their daughter and Whit good evening.

"Happy?"

Whit pulled her into his arms, relishing the feel of her against him. He had wanted to hold her all day.

"Ecstatic." Her response was muffled as she burrowed her head into his chest. "I've been wanting you and my parents to meet for ages."

"Your dad is really interesting. I enjoyed visiting with him. And your mom is a sweetheart. I could tell they're both anxious to see that my intentions toward you are strictly honorable."

"Are they?" Terra joked, trying to sound like a doting Victorian matron. "Are your intentions honorable, sir?"

Whit's look was intense, serious.

"The ball is in your court, Terra. You tell me how fast or how slow to go, and I'll follow. It's got to be obvious to you that I love you."

She had thought so.

She had hoped so.

So what was it, she worried, that kept her from telling him what "honorable intentions" meant to her? They meant marriage, didn't they?

Of course, Terra answered herself. She wasn't a woman who would settle for less than marriage, when she knew it was right. And this feeling she had for Whit was very right.

"Let's take things slowly, Whit. We need time to really get to know each other. I want you to really know me, to know what you're getting into," she joked. "I heard you arguing politics with my mom. That's a good start."

She threaded her arms around his neck and lay her head on his shoulder. He was comfortable. Solid.

"Now it's your turn." Whit pulled back from her, looking into her eyes with the intensity she had seen when he was dancing at the Powwow.

"My turn?"

"Tomorrow, there's a tribal feast on the reservation. My

whole family will be there. I told them we'd be there around noon.''

Color drained from Terra's lips as she backed away from the sanctuary of Whit's arms.

''No.''

''No, what?''

''No, I can't go to the reservation, Whit.'' Her words, though softly spoken, echoed discordantly in the silence of the room.

''Other plans?'' He feared the answer before it came.

''No. But I can't go to the reservation.''

''Can't . . . or won't?''

She saw the muscle in his jaw clench as his teeth ground together in frustration. His eyes, uncompromising and hard, drilled into hers.

''You know how I feel about it, Whit. Someone on that reservation handed over a tiny baby to total strangers. That baby was me. I can't get over that.''

''You're going to have to, Terra. You're going to have to face the fact and move on. Because that reservation is an important part of my life. It's home to me. No matter where I go, I'll always come back there. I told you before, a Crow always comes home. If you're going to be part of my life—and I want with all my heart for you to be— sometime you're going to have to go with me.''

''I'll be here waiting when you come back.'' Her shoulders flexed defensively. She knew it was small consolation, but it was all she could offer.

He paced the floor like a caged animal.

She stood statue-still, her eyes following his steps.

He stopped, keeping a distance between them.

His voice was low, almost a growl. ''You come with me tomorrow, Terra. I've met your family. If my mom's broken leg hadn't kept them from the Powwow, you would've met mine tonight, too. But I'm going to see them tomorrow. Come with me. Do me the honor of meeting my people.''

"I can't," she repeated. "I'll see you when you get back."

The walls were silent. Terra felt like she could hear the paint on the ceiling, the room was so quiet.

"If you don't come to the reservation with me tomorrow, Terra"—his words were spoken slowly, definitively—"I won't be back."

The finality of his words struck her like a blow.

"Is this more important to you than I am?" She felt hot tears surging down her cheeks. She hated her loss of control, but she hated his words more.

"What's important," he said patiently, "is getting to know each other, so our love can have a foundation. I want this to last forever, Terra. But you'll never really know me until you see where I came from. Who I am. Who my family is. And more than that . . ." His hand reached out to her, but he deliberately avoided touching her. ". . . who you really are. You are a Crow woman, Terra. Nothing will change that."

"I will not go."

Whit's ashen face reflected his inner agony. "You know, Terra, when I was growing up, I experienced fear and hatred from small-minded bigots who never tried to understand the Indian ways. But I didn't expect to find prejudice in the woman I love. If you so fear our people, Terra, yours and mine, there's no future for us. If you won't go to the reservation with me, I can't come back to you."

Words failed her. The ultimatum had been issued. An emotional abyss had split the earth between them, leaving him on one shore while she stood, agonized, on the opposite side.

The sequence of his leaving replayed over and over in her head all night: grabbing his jacket, storming out the door and slamming it loudly, stomping down the stairs, grinding the gears on his borrowed car, squealing tires as he shot away from the curb. The condo felt so empty, echoing with his memory. The only sound she couldn't hear was the shattering of her heart as it broke in two.

Chapter Five

The rain-swollen Missouri River slapped against its grassy banks, gurgling and churning in a hasty journey downstream. Mottled shadows filtering through overhanging cottonwood branches danced across the meadow. Native range grasses provided a startling green contrast to the crimson Indian paintbrushes and yellow roosterheads blooming in profusion.

The sun was high in the western sky. The afternoon's heat brought deerflies out in force. They droned in the sunlight and lingered, uninvited and unappreciated, around the chestnut gelding's flanks. The horse flicked his tail sporadically, switching pesky insects from his hide.

"Whoa, boy." Terra reined him to a halt at the water's edge. In one smooth motion, she slid from the saddle and tethered the horse on a high spot at the edge of the wetlands area.

The flaxen-maned horse nibbled at the low-growing vegetation and pulled a mouthful of grass. A five-year veteran of the FWP Department, the horse had participated in more field studies than most of the administrators behind desks had experienced. He was a good horse, sleek and strong. And the fact that his hooves left less impact on this portion of sensitive range than a truck's tires would produce made him an important part of the survey team.

While most of Montana's wildlife species were plentiful and healthy, some needed special management and protection. Two of the wetlands plants—the water howellia and

Ute ladies' tresses—were under protection status. Each May, Terra rode out through the sensitive wetlands area to survey the plants. Habitat studies were part of each FWP worker's role.

In states with larger budgets, plant specialists would be on the payroll. Due to the relatively small staff in Montana, however, game management officers doubled as plant surveyors as they conducted habitat studies this time of the year. The wetlands plants were, after all, part of the wildlife of the region.

Summer was in its infancy in the Big Sky State. The air held the rich aroma of fresh grass, of sun-warmed soil, of life renewed.

The silence of the wetlands, punctuated only by the call of resident birds and the buzz of curious insects, was a welcome relief. After spending three days in the office, being away from the jangling phones and endless office chatter was heavenly.

Now, Terra had time to think, time to enjoy her work as she had always enjoyed it before.

She flipped her field notebook open and prepared to list the managed plants in a designated quadrant.

A faint murmur caught her attention.

In the sun-kissed, sprawling meadow, it was quiet enough to hear her own heartbeat. It pounded like an Indian drum, steady and strong.

Anyone coming across the woman at that moment would've seen her lips lose their color, her eyes grow haunted and sad.

In the weeks since Whit had stormed out of her condo, she had thrown herself even more deeply into her work than usual, and had ignored the feeling of complete and utter loss that had dogged her every moment. It wasn't just missing his phone calls or his faxes and letters, nor was it the lack of flowers being delivered to the office.

It was his smile.

The way he ran his thumb over hers when they held hands.

It was the overwhelming sense of emptiness, knowing she wouldn't be telling him tonight how wildly beautiful the river had looked this afternoon.

He wouldn't hear that she had helped with a mule deer count last week, or that she and Pam had conducted a Wildlife in Montana Schools classroom visit last month.

He wouldn't know she had lost nine pounds, or that she had bought a new Waylon Jennings CD.

She'd have to water her own plants, and they wouldn't receive the loving attention—the meaningful conversation between him and his petunias, he called it—the way he jokingly greeted each one when he visited her condo.

Like minor-key music, he was haunting and beautiful and different. His smile constantly sang in her head.

Mostly, Terra realized as tears inundated her notebook, blurring her field notes, he wouldn't know that walking out the door, he had taken her heart with him.

Tears that had been pushed deep inside her for too long now surfaced. Everything that had bothered her for years suddenly erupted. Once the tears started, they overflowed.

Tears for the pain of not having Whit's arms to fly to for comfort.

Tears for the beautifully free wolf, shot and left dead in the ice on the Madison River bank.

Tears for the tiny Crow baby whose mother handed her over to strangers.

Tears of disappointment in herself. She had never been afraid of anything, or anyone, before. Nor had she distrusted another human being. Even her birth mother, she realized at that moment, should be allowed to explain the reason for the adoption.

Crying was cathartic. There was something satisfying about crying herself silly, something good about getting red puffy eyes and a runny nose.

It was an accomplishment, she realized, like a nice

sneeze, only more so. It was also completely ridiculous. That realization only made her cry more.

It was also, Terra scolded herself, completely unlike her. She fought to regain control.

And when the tears had all been shed, and the colorful endangered flowers had been chronicled, Terra dried her eyes and flipped her notebook closed.

The afternoon's work was complete. In the process, an idea had flowered in her mind, merely a bud of a thought that began to blossom as she loaded the horse trailer and steered the truck onto the highway. By the time she had returned to the office, the idea was in full bloom. It would be cultivated, like any growing thing, until the idea was ready for harvest.

It was nearly nine that night when Terra arrived and searched the noisy, smoke-filled club for Pam and their friend, Heather Chambers. At a table scarcely bigger than a pizza, the two women, along with three men whom Terra hadn't met, were huddled in deep conversation.

"Hey, guys!" Terra's greeting prompted one of the men to rise and offer a chair.

She smiled her thanks and sat down. Introductions circled the table. Two of the men were with the Mountain West Bank; the third was the youngest generation of an old-line law firm that had operated in central Montana for nearly a century.

Open Microphone Night at the club afforded an opportunity for new talent to showcase their skills. As cappuccino carafes were passed, Terra's group watched a young comedian fire off his raunchy routine to a lukewarm audience.

The next act, a stocky cowboy with far more whiskers than talent, moaned into the mike while strumming an acoustic guitar badly in need of tuning.

"So much for his unplugged performance." Pam

laughed. "The real shame is, the audience's ears were unplugged!"

Terra recognized the grocery store checker who then took the spotlight. Shrink-wrapped in luminescent spandex leggings and two-thirds of a blouse, the blond fluffed her already-massive hair and began fiddling with the microphone. She bent it in one direction, pouted, stepped up to it, then stepped back again. After going through the same ritual two more times, she stepped forward, cleared her throat, and sang. Loudly. Not well, but very loudly.

Following her, an unshaven man in wrinkled, baggy clothes recited a poem which had no rhyme but lots of sentiment for his long-lost pet iguana.

"Remind me why I came here tonight?" Terra threw out the question to Pam.

"You've been blue since you broke up with Whit," was Pam's ready answer. "You needed cheering up."

A discount Dolly Parton and a poem about a lost lizard. Cheering up indeed, Terra thought.

"Forget the cappuccino. We're going to need a pot of real coffee to get through this," Pam warned the group. "But I refuse to leave before I give all this raw talent a chance."

The simultaneous groans around the table brought the first real laughter of the evening.

"Hey! I've heard this guy before," Heather pointed out as the next performer took his place at the mike. "He's great."

"Especially on the eyes," Pam put in.

"You're a pushover for a good-looking guy in a cowboy hat," Heather challenged her.

Pam grinned and nodded, flashing her friends the thumbs-up sign. Yep, they had her pegged.

The reed-thin cowboy stepped up on the bandstand and flicked the brim of his hat back with one finger. He squinted past the stage lights into the crowd, then adjusted the strap on his guitar and plucked at the strings. His voice, clear and mellow, was not unlike George Strait's as he began his introduction.

"Here's a song I wrote last year, and the local radio stations have been giving it a little airtime, for which I'm real grateful." His smile didn't reach all the way to his eyes. The song opened:

> *I should have walked away*
> *Before we danced together,*
> *Before you ever felt*
> *The hunger in my touch.*
>
> *I wouldn't have to live*
> *Just this side of heartbreak,*
> *If I had never known*
> *I could love someone this much.*

As the ballad's first notes drifted across the room, the audience quieted down, noticeably attentive to his smooth delivery.

Terra felt the words reach inside her and twist her heart with familiarity. This was the song that had been playing from the lounge of the Mountain Crest Inn the first night she and Whit had gone out to dinner.

"Have you ever felt that way about anybody?" Whit had asked her.

"No," Terra had replied honestly. She'd never known that kind of love.

Not until she fell in love with Whit, she now corrected herself.

In the hush that had fallen over the audience in the smoky club, she listened as the cowboy sang the chorus:

> *I'll go back to my world,*
> *To my familiar place*
> *Where every time I look for you,*
> *I won't see your face.*

But still I won't forget you,
Even when you're not around
'Cause just this side of heartbreak
Your memory still is found.

It was as though it were written for her, expressing her longing so completely. It was her story, since Whit had walked out.

Did she miss him more when she was alone, she wondered, or with a group of people? It didn't seem to matter. Her mind couldn't shake him for more than a minute regardless of what she was doing, what else she was thinking.

Would it be this way the rest of her life? Would the gut-wrenching sensation of loss never leave her?

The audience's appreciation of the performer was evident in the hearty applause sweeping across the room. The cowboy tipped his hat and ambled from the stage in long, lanky strides. A three-piece combo loaded their equipment on the bandstand for the next round of entertainment.

"I think I'll be going now," Terra told no one in particular at the table. Pam and Heather were deeply engrossed in their dates; the third man was trying to catch his reflection in the mirror over the bar, when he wasn't blowing smoke in everybody's face.

"Stick around." The lawyer squinted between puffs, his cigarette bobbing up and down from his lips like a railroad semaphore. "I'll let you talk me into a dance."

Oh, do me an honor, she thought sarcastically.

"Thanks, no." Terra shook her head. "I really have to be going."

She rose from her chair and in the smoke-enshrouded neon light wove through the crowded tables to the door.

The early summer evening was cool and pine-scented. Hovering above the silhouetted mountains, the moon was a sliver of gold. She paused for a moment, enjoying the respite from the smoky, noisy darkness inside.

"Beautiful evening, isn't it?" Startled by the voice behind her, she swung around. In the faint moonlight, leaning against the backdoor frame of the club, the cowboy singer stood with a lazy grin. His arms were folded across his chest nonchalantly: he clearly didn't give a darn about most anything.

"That it is," she agreed with a smile. "I enjoyed your song."

He raised a hand to his hat brim in gallant salute. "Thank you kindly, ma'am." He gestured toward a picnic bench in the garden adjacent to the club's parking lot. "Would you care to sit a spell? I have to go back in there and sing during the second set, but I need to breathe some air I can't see."

"I know what you mean." She was in total agreement. "It sure gets smoky in there. I'm glad I didn't leave earlier, though, or I'd have missed your song. Have you written others?"

"A couple more. Nothing I've recorded. That one is my favorite, though. I wrote it last year when I thought I was gonna die of a broken heart." His laugh was sardonic. "But I survived and so did the song."

"You wrote it from personal experience?" *So I'm not the only person who's ever been steamrollered by love.* Terra took little comfort in that realization.

The singer nodded. "I fell in love with a beautiful little gal who wanted me to quit rodeoing and go back to college. I couldn't do it. I always had to hit the road one more time to chase my own tail. I went from Cheyenne to Reno to Calgary while she waited for me. In Oklahoma, I drew a bull nobody could ride. But I sure as heck tried. I saw stars for about a week after he threw me. What the old bull did manage to do, though, was knock some sense into my thick skull. I packed my gear and drove back to Montana to be with her."

"Good." Terra heard herself voice encouragement.

"Problem was"—the cowboy shook his head—"she was gone when I got back. Seems I'd left her waiting one too many times. It's pretty crazy, isn't it? I was so afraid of her world, and now I'd give most everything I've got to be there.''

''Pretty crazy.'' Terra wasn't sure which of them she was describing: the singer or herself. There was no agony like being a world away from somebody you love. ''But maybe she'll take you back.''

''I doubt that she would.'' The cowboy shook his head and snorted. ''And I'm pretty sure the guy she married last month wouldn't like it none either.''

The thump of bass guitars from inside the clubhouse pulsated even in the parking lot. Farther down the highway, a truck's jake brakes clattered in the night.

''I'm sorry.'' Terra meant it. He seemed like a nice guy.

''Stupid pride. I shoulda come down off my high horse and realized how little she was askin'. And I realize now, she wasn't askin' it for herself. She knew it was for my own good.''

As she drove away from the clubhouse, the cowboy's words bounced around in Terra's head. *''Stupid pride . . . how little she was asking . . . for my own good.''*

The night was too beautiful, and her emotions were too far into overdrive, to go straight home. She missed Whit with an intensity that scared her.

She turned on Ten Mile Creek Road and headed up Schuster Canyon. The black dark of the national forest was magically relaxing. Parking her truck, she stepped out and drank in the heady fragrance of pine, the spicy tingle of fir.

The night air held a bite even in summer. Her shoulders shook down a shiver as she turned to open her pickup door.

Near the foot of the mountain, past the campground road darting off to her right, Terra caught a glimmer of light.

Getting into her truck, she neglected to turn on her headlights while she sat, watching.

The light appeared again, flickering through the dense stand of timber, then went out.

Terra hit the ignition switch on her truck. It clicked like a schoolmarm tsking her disapproval.

Better get a new starter, Terra warned herself, *before I find myself stranded when the truck doesn't start.*

She looked again toward the spot in the forest. It was dark now. The elusive light was extinguished.

Strange, she thought. Campgrounds in this area wouldn't open until after Memorial Day. That was a week away. And Forest Service crews wouldn't be working at this time of the night.

Nancy Bartlett snapped the tattered woolen blanket over her bedding plants in the darkened backyard, and let it flutter down to cover them against the frost predicted to hit during the night. The third week in May was really too early to be setting out plants in Montana. Yet she always rushed the season. The pansies would make it without cover, hardy little beasts that they were. But the impatiens were no match against the gnashing, vicious teeth of frost. Lobelia, alyssum, dianthus . . . they all needed covering tonight.

"Mason," she called from the back porch, "did you talk to Terra today?"

"Called the office. She was out doing habitat studies. There was a message on the answering machine when I got home. Said she was going out with Pam and Heather tonight."

"I worry." Nancy poked her head in the back door. "She's been so quiet since she broke up with her fellow."

"She's a grown woman," Mason admonished his wife. "She has to work it out on her own." He folded his history book on his lap and stared off into the room. All the years of love and care couldn't help Terra now. She had to decide for herself what to do.

He knew what the problem was. Despite their offers over the years to help find her birth parents, Terra had refused. He knew it ate at her, the circumstances of her birth. He wished he could help. But the information they'd gotten from the Department of Social Services was sketchy. All they knew, they had told her. But it wasn't enough. And that had become a problem for Terra.

Mason stared at her high school graduation picture on the wall. His little girl. Did every dad feel the overwhelming sense of love and protection he held for his two kids? Probably.

But this was something she had to work out on her own. He couldn't fix it. Only Terra could.

As if by telepathy, the phone jangled at that very moment.

"Hi, princess." Nancy heard her husband's greeting. It would be Terra calling. "Your mother was just wondering about you. Here, let me put her on."

Nancy stepped out of her scruffy outdoor shoes and crossed the carpet to take the phone.

"Hello, dear."

"Mom," Terra's voice was pensive, "are you available for lunch tomorrow? I need to talk to you about something."

"Meet me at Chandler's at noon?" Nancy knew the restaurant was Terra's favorite.

"Thanks, Mom. You're the best."

The clatter of dishes mingled with the lunchtime crowd's conversations to create a cacophony of noise in the fern-filled eatery at the edge of the pedestrian mall.

Nancy lovingly watched her daughter enter the restaurant, scan the crowd, and smile when she spotted her mother. She crossed the room in quick strides.

The girl never did anything slowly, Nancy thought to herself. It was always full speed ahead for Terra, who never found enough hours in the day to accomplish all the things that interested her.

"Hi, Mums." Terra bent and hugged the older woman before taking her seat. "Thanks for coming."

"Wouldn't miss the chance," Nancy teased. "We don't see much of you these days."

"Busy time at work. That time of year." Terra scanned the menu and followed Nancy's order with her own when the waitress appeared.

Maybe it wasn't any busier time than usual, Nancy guessed. Maybe it was just that Terra felt the need to fill the hours with work. A mind full of work might prevent thoughts of Whitman Bull Chief from entering. Still, Nancy knew it was futile for Terra to quit thinking about him. She knew the girl had agonized over their breakup.

Small talk was not either woman's habit. Nancy zeroed in on the target as she addressed her daughter.

"Dear, you wanted to talk to me about something important. I could tell it in your voice when you called. What is it?"

The younger woman's sigh was ragged. She looked directly at her mother. Nancy's sandy brown hair—hair with little gray—skimmed the collar of her smartly tailored suit. Her smile folded into smooth pink cheeks. A casual observer could plausibly mistake the attractive mother-daughter pair for sisters.

I want to be like you, Terra realized. *I want to look like you. Why can't I be really your daughter, and not any other woman's child?*

It was frightening, what she was about to ask. Still, her life couldn't move forward until the idea that had taken root was allowed to bloom.

"You've always told me you would help me if I asked you. Now I'm asking. I need to know about my birth parents."

From the time they had brought their baby girl home, Nancy had known this day might come.

"I see." The smoothness in Nancy's voice belied the trembling in her stomach. She folded her napkin on the table and ran her thumbnail along the crease. If her hands stayed busy, she reasoned, they wouldn't shake. "How can your dad and I help?"

"Tell me what you know about my biological mother."

Nancy's hand ceased its attention to the linen napkin, and moved on. She stirred her tea slowly, each click of the spoon against the cup resounding in her head like a heartbeat.

"We know," she began, "she's a Crow Indian woman from the reservation. We weren't told her age, or the circumstances of your birth. We wanted you so badly. . . ." Nancy's voice trailed off.

"Did you . . . did you specifically ask for an Indian baby?" Terra stifled a sob. She felt exposed. Raw. And terribly vulnerable.

Nancy shook her head, her lips curved into a tight, melancholy smile. "When we applied for adoption, we didn't specify anything but a baby. We didn't care whether we got a boy or girl, what color, what size, it didn't matter. Your dad and I had so much love to share with a baby. That's all that mattered to us then, and it's still all that matters. You are our daughter."

"So you weren't disappointed that I wasn't blond and blue-eyed?"

"Are you kidding?" Nancy looked incredulous. "You were our baby from the moment they placed you in my arms. Your dad and I felt all the love in the world when we looked at you. Nothing will ever change that."

Tears threatened to spill from her dark eyes as Terra held her mother's trembling hand.

"I want to search for the people who gave me up, Mom. Nobody'll ever be my parents but you and Dad. Please understand that. But until I get settled in my own mind what happened in my past, I can't contemplate my future. Do you know what I mean?"

"Terra, are you doing this because of Whit?"

"No," she answered instantly. Her voice was firm. "He won't know about this. Maybe he wouldn't even care. He doesn't intend to come back to me, Mother. He made that clear. But no, I'm not doing this for him. It's something I can't quit thinking about, so I'm going to have to face it. I'm doing it for me.''

Chapter Six

William Mason Bartlett shuffled through the papers in his briefcase, setting aside the ruled yellow tablet and well-chewed pencils that accompanied him everywhere. Paper-clipped to the pocket of the case was a snapshot of Jennifer and the twins. How those babies had grown in the six weeks since that picture was taken!

Retrieving an envelope from the slew of paperwork awaiting his attention, he closed the case and set it beside his home-office desk.

It had been a long day. He and Jennifer, with the twins in tow, had taken Terra sight-seeing around New Orleans. His sister had only a week's vacation to spend with them. He wanted it to be packed with fun.

The drone of the air conditioner cut through the silence of the night. The attorney checked his wristwatch. It was after midnight. He should be in bed. He tapped the corner of the envelope on the desk, feeling the letter inside shift with each tap.

A client wishing to locate her birth parents . . . that was how Willy had phrased his request to the Montana Department of Social Services. An unidentified client. Not: his sister, his best friend, his lifelong buddy. Just some nameless, faceless adoptee searching for her past.

If Terra changed her mind, if she realized the potential for heartache in searching out her birth parents and decided against it, Willy would support her decision. In practicing law, he had represented clients who sought their birth par-

79

ents. Sometimes the results were jubilation; sometimes the misery outweighed the end result. But either way, Willy would be there for his sister.

The last time she had needed his help was when she was eight years old and couldn't reach the top shelf of the closet where they knew Christmas presents were hidden. Her independence grew as she did.

Willy wondered now, had she ever really needed anybody in her life? She prided herself on her independence.

Yes, he answered himself, she needed him, and their parents, more than ever.

The cool waterfront of Lake Pontchartrain at sunset was a welcome relief from the day's cloying heat as Terra strolled with her brother. They had devoured Creole delicacies, toured the Superdome, and listened to great jazz in the French Quarter.

Whit didn't like jazz, she remembered. If they were here together, she'd be happy listening to music he liked. She'd be happy with him, period.

Jennifer had taken the twins home for a nap, affording her husband the opportunity to spend time alone with his sister.

The Rivertown Aquarium tour pushed Terra into work mode. She studied the fishery displays with rapt interest, taking mental notes on incorporating some of the exhibit ideas back home in Montana.

In another part of the museum, Native American exhibits drew their attention. A tall, leather-clad mannequin elicited Willy's surprised response.

"That's an authentic, antique leather shirt," he pointed out. "Look at the size of it. Can you imagine somebody with shoulders that broad?"

Yes, I can, Terra thought. No imagination was necessary. The last broad shoulders she'd seen in fringed buckskin belonged to Whit. In the weeks since the Powwow, in the days since arriving in New Orleans, she'd never stopped thinking about him.

Willy caught the look in her eyes, the hurt as she quietly answered, "Yes."

Their mother had warned him on the phone before Terra arrived, not to mention Whit. The breakup of his sister's romance, as Nancy referred to it, had left the girl at loose ends. The trip to New Orleans was the best thing in the world for Terra, Nancy assured her son.

"Hey," Willy nudged her. "Let's go ride a riverboat."

The *Mississippi Princess* was already loading passengers when they scurried across the dock, purchased tickets, and boarded the famous steamboat. Overhead, the discordant calliope music was drowned out by earsplitting blasts from twin stacks, signaling the boat's departure.

"Let's go on the top deck," Willy suggested. "We can see clear down the river from up there."

The Mississippi River held its own particular fascination: the troutlines and water hyacinth dotting its edges, the egrets and cranes standing like sentinels along the banks, the tugs and barges conducting their business.

The sun was relentlessly bright. Tourists with neck-strapped cameras focused and clicked enthusiastically as the huge boat took the first bend and headed up the river.

Willy brought two Cokes to the table and clicked his waxed cup against his sister's.

"To your good health, Sis."

"And yours," she smiled as she returned his toast.

"Having fun?"

"Absolutely." She meant it. Good times were always better when Willy was around. They were inseparable as youngsters, and the two people's friendship had deepened with age.

"Got something I want to talk to you about." Willy's gaze scanned the riverbank. He'd never really appreciated the diversity of wildlife along the river until today, never noticed the variety of birds until Terra pointed them out to him.

"Talk away." His sister grinned.

"I've checked on adoption laws in Montana. Each state's are different, you know."

"And?"

"They sent me the agenda to follow in searching for your birth parents."

Terra's eyes went dark. Whether from suspicion or just from the glaring sunlight on the upper deck, Willy couldn't say.

"What do I do?" Her question hovered in the air between them like a dragonfly.

"First, you need to know that in Montana, adoption records are kept confidential. So we need—"

"We? You'll help me, Willy?"

He nodded. "Of course. So we need," he continued, "to petition the court to appoint an intermediary. This person will work between you and the birth parents and determine whether they are willing to have the file opened to you."

"Do you mean this intermediary—this total stranger—can have access to information telling who my parents are, but I can't?" Terra hated the shrillness in her voice, but was helpless to prevent it.

"I'm afraid so. But let's think positive, Sis. If the birth parents, or their legal representative, allow the file to be opened, you'll be able to identify them."

"Then what?" *Help me, Willy, I've never been so scared.*

Scared of finding out who I am.

Scared of not finding out.

Scared of why they gave me away.

"Then it's up to you, what you do next. You can contact them . . ." Willy's voice took on his professional, attorney-at-law tone. ". . . or not. That's your choice."

"If it were you, would you want to know, Wills?"

He thought for only a moment.

"What I want doesn't matter here." His voice was gentle, patient. "Only you can make that decision, Terra. You'll have to decide for yourself."

An old saying rattled around in Montana: Summer doesn't come until the snow leaves the mountains, and snow doesn't leave the mountains until summer comes. Grandma Bartlett had repeated the old adage to Terra every spring. The dear old woman had been gone ten years now. Still, Terra smiled at her memory as the plane descended near Sacajewea Peak and made its final approach to the airport. The mountains were green and devoid of snow. Summer had at last arrived in the Big Sky Country.

Pam was waiting inside the terminal, facetiously holding a hand-lettered sign that read, *What did you bring me?*

"I brought you an Elvis mug for your new collection." Terra grinned as they climbed into Pam's car. She had nearly brought her friend another snowglobe, but remembered they were last month's collection. Snowglobes out, Elvis mugs in. What Pam lacked in stability of collections, however, she more than compensated for in kindness. Terra treasured their close friendship.

"Sweet!" Pam declared. "I can't wait to see it."

"So fill me in on work, even though I really don't want to think about my vacation being over."

"We've been swamped with game survey work," Pam volunteered. "And of course the bison situation has become a nationwide issue. What a nightmare! We were the headliner on CNN last night."

Bison suspected of carrying the dreaded brucellosis virus were being shot as they left the confines of Yellowstone National Park. A highly controversial program, it had drawn fire from animal rights groups and others who denounced the move. The huge beasts were being slaughtered by the hundreds. They were just so many unsuspecting pawns in a political game of chess.

"I'll bet Max is fit to be tied!" Terra knew her supervisor's dedication to his job eschewed any criticism of the Fish, Wildlife & Parks Department's actions.

"Well, he's been so busy this past week, he hasn't had time to worry about it," Pam responded, preoccupied with navigating through rush-hour traffic from the airport. "The Feds have been here all week."

The minute the words came out, Pam regretted them. One of those Feds, as she had always nicknamed the group of advisers from Washington, D.C., had the power to break Terra's heart, and he had done just that.

The car's air conditioner hummed softly.

No other sound penetrated the silence of the sedan.

Pam wove from the passing lane to choke off a cattle truck. An angry horn blared as she accelerated and relegated the stock truck to a rapidly fading image in her rear-view mirror.

"Is Whit here?"

The question came out of its own volition. Terra hadn't wanted to ask it.

"Yes," Pam answered simply, "he is."

"Are their meetings continuing tomorrow?" Terra feared her friend's answer.

"All day tomorrow, and Friday, too."

Allergies and onions couldn't bring on tears any faster than just thinking of Whit did. Terra felt her eyes filling up, threatening to spill over.

"You don't have to see him, honey." Pam agonized over the torment on her friend's face. *Why can't Whitman Bull Chief stay in his fancy office in Washington, D.C.?* she thought angrily. *Why does he have to show up here and walk all over Terra's heart with his expensive, Italian leather shoes?*

"But what if I do?" Terra's voice quivered. "I can't even think about him without shaking, Pam."

"They'll be in meetings all day. You'll be out on the range. There's no reason your paths should cross."

No reason at all.

So when their paths did in fact cross the next evening, Terra could only cuss herself for not being prepared for the sight of him.

She had left the truck in the service garage with the keys in it, following the procedure the department used when a vehicle needed routine maintenance. Crossing the lawn to her own truck parked in front of the office, she glanced up to see him.

Was it only the magic of mountain twilight, Terra wondered, that painted him in golden half-light . . . that turned his dark eyes to diamonds . . . that intensified the lithe, cougarlike grace of his stride?

A gentle breeze lifted an errant strand of her hair, and she pushed it back impatiently.

"Hello, Terra."

His voice, as smooth as it had been in her dreams, was low, melodic.

Don't cry, Terra admonished herself. Her eyes blinked back tears she was afraid to shed, and ached like the rest of her.

Stop shaking.

Stop clicking your thumbnails together.

Get your head up. Don't let him know you're dying inside.

"Hi, Whit."

They stood in the middle of the green grass, sheltered by towering pine trees.

Had he grown even more handsome? Yes, she thought, he had.

His dreams hadn't deceived him, Whit realized. She was really as beautiful as the image of her which had haunted his sleep since he last saw her.

"How have you been?"

His seemingly innocuous question angered her. How had she been? She had been lousy, thank you very much, since he walked out of her life.

She had been reduced to weeping on a riverbank, a

woman whose fiercely protected independence had suddenly meant no more than a dandelion seed wafting on the summer breeze.

Her life had been miserably empty without him. That's how she'd been. She missed him so much her teeth hurt.

"Great." She forced a smile and tossed her head defiantly. "Just great."

"Terra?"

"Yes?"

"Do me a favor?" A suggestion of impatience rippled the muscles under his trimly tailored white shirt. His breathing was labored, agitated.

Anything, she wanted to answer him. But she made herself remain cool. Nothing would be gained by letting him see her heartache.

Her face reflected her confusion. "What favor?"

"The next time the Red Cross has a blood drawing in town, go down and donate some of those ice cubes in your veins." His cynical tone surprised her.

"What's that supposed to mean?" The shock of his uncharacteristic sarcasm shrilled her voice.

"It means I never knew you could be so cold, so uncaring." He reached out and took hold of her wrist, holding it lightly. "I wanted us to be together."

Terra heard herself give a short, bitter laugh, harsh even to her own ears.

"On your terms, Whit? With you setting the parameters as to what control I have over my life? No thanks. I want love on equal terms, not someone dictating to me how I'm supposed to feel, someone walking out on me because I can't feel what he's feeling. You should've understood that." She glared down at his hand, until he removed it from her wrist.

Willing her knees not to collapse, she walked quickly past him. She had to get away, before he could see the tears in her eyes, before he could hear the pain in her voice.

He turned and spoke to her back as she escaped down

the sidewalk, leaving with the picture of him: tall, incredibly handsome, and alone.

"Good-bye, Terra."

Four weeks into June, vegetable plants were sprouting in the mountain-high gardens of Montana. The nights were, for the most part, past the danger of frost. Old-timers, however, warned that killing frosts on the Fourth of July were not unheard of. With an average growing season of only eighty-nine days, gardening at this altitude was both challenging and rewarding.

Nancy Bartlett tended to her rows of vegetables almost as lovingly as she had raised her children. Nearly every week now, Terra joined her mother in the backyard to wage their war against quack grass and chickweeds.

Game animals had moved to their summer range, relishing the abundant grass of open meadows. The rivers were at last running free, the last vestiges of winter ice now only a memory.

Tourism, rapidly becoming one of Montana's leading industries, flourished. Gas prices at the pumps had been pushed up three, five, eight cents a gallon, reflecting the influx of out-of-state vacationers.

Following a full day of game tracking, Terra returned to her condo hoping for a cool shower and a light dinner before going to bed. It had been a warm day. She wore layers of sweat, dust, and weariness like a suit. As she unlocked the door, the ringing phone greeted her.

It would prove to be the call she had both anticipated and feared. The intermediary appointed by the court had acted on her petition.

"Is there a convenient time for us to meet and review my findings?" The woman's approach was professional, her voice impersonal.

Terra scanned the week on her desk calendar. Tomorrow she'd be in the office. It was simply a matter of arranging a couple of hours off. Agreeing on a time, the women each thanked the other and hung up.

Ella Williams appeared at Terra's condo promptly at three the next afternoon. In her conservative suit and no-nonsense shoes, she was the very picture of efficiency.

She had conducted hundreds of these meetings; at most of them, she was met with trepidation as adoptees awaited word on the status of their petitions.

After social pleasantries had been exchanged, Terra braced herself and asked the question that had hung over her like a shroud for weeks.

"Ms. Williams, have you met with my birth parents?"

The woman watched a range of emotions splash across Terra Bartlett's face: curiosity, fear, hope, irresolution.

Terra realized she would never want to play poker with this woman, whose face bore no expression.

"I have," the intermediary answered after a moment's hesitation, "met with the legal representative for your birth parents."

"Legal representative?" The tremor in Terra's voice was uncontrollable. "Why didn't my birth parents represent themselves?"

"You'll have to contact this person for your answers, Ms. Bartlett." Handing Terra an envelope, the woman rose and started toward the door. She turned. An enigmatic smile washed across her face. "I hope you'll find the answers you're seeking, Ms. Bartlett. Good luck."

Long after the woman left, Terra stared at the envelope. It was almost ludicrous, this feeling of power. After years of wondering about her origin, the envelope in her shaking hands held the information she needed.

She peeled a corner of the sealed envelope back and slowly tore a jagged line across the flap. The heavy vellum letter lay folded within. Reverently removing it, Terra sat down and began to read the document.

Amid the legal jargon covering the page was the information Terra was searching for. Her eyes locked on it.

Mrs. Neva Old Elk, it read, had been appointed as legal representative for Raymond and Terisa Light.

Raymond and Terisa, Terra read again. *My birth parents.*

Raymond and Terisa. Real people. People with a baby named Terra.

Except that they wouldn't keep their baby, and now they wouldn't legally represent themselves.

The cowards, Terra thought venomously. Their sheer lack of responsibility astounded her. Did she even want to know anyone like that?

No.

Yes.

She must know more. Her life was like a fragmented jigsaw puzzle, with multisided pieces lying in wait to complete the picture.

Folding the letter resolutely, she stuffed it into the torn envelope. Her mind was made up.

Mrs. Neva Old Elk, look out. I'm coming to see you, and I'm coming with questions. And I'm not leaving until I get answers.

Terra spread the highway map across her kitchen table and smoothed it out. Here—she pointed with one finger— was Blue Rock, where Whit's family lived, on the edge of the Crow Reservation. And here—she spanned the distance and marked it with her thumb—was Staghorn, on the opposite side of the reservation near its eastern border.

She read the letter again. Mrs. Neva Old Elk, Staghorn, Montana. Staghorn was nearly three hours away by interstate. If Terra called her tonight maybe, just maybe, she could drive over there this weekend.

"I'm sorry," the nasal-toned voice in Directory Assistance droned, "I don't show a listing for that name."

Great. Back to square one. Wherever square one was.

I've come this far. I've got to follow through, Terra pledged. Showing up uninvited on Neva Old Elk's doorstep would breach all rules of etiquette, yet Terra knew she wouldn't be a complete surprise. After all, the court-appointed intermediary had obviously contacted the woman. Neva Old Elk knew Terra would be looking for her.

It's not like I want to embarrass her by suddenly appearing in her life, Terra reasoned. *Heck, I'm too big to be left on her doorstep in a basket.*

Folding the map, her decision was cemented. Friday after work, she'd drive to Staghorn.

With less than an hour until sunset, the western sky was streaked purple and orange. The sun, a glowing red ball, hung suspended above the horizon, descending slowly toward the serenity of the distant hills.

Grasshoppers flying erratically from lush wheat fields collided with the tires and clicked against her truck as Terra turned off the highway onto the dusty county road. She had passed through Blue Rock an hour ago but neglected to stop in town. Not knowing where Whit's family lived made it easier to dismiss him from her thoughts, she believed. That he had stayed on her mind all the way to Staghorn discounted that theory.

Driving through each dale and around each bend, Terra pictured a young Whit running across the fields, his dog in hot pursuit, as they lived the idyllic childhood he had described.

It was beautiful country, different from the mountains she called home, but vast and majestic. Cereal grains undulated in the scant breeze. Pastures with every color of horse rolled toward the horizon. It was a serene, tranquil place.

The reflective sign marking the entrance to Staghorn glinted in the setting sun.

This is it, Terra knew. *No turning back.*

On the left, the Staghorn Elementary School sat quietly amidst bark-covered playgrounds. With school just dismissed for the summer, it would be two months before activity would again enliven the swing sets, monkey bars, and tetherball courts.

A convenience store with gas pumps in front sat ahead on her right. Terra steered between them and rolled to a stop.

" 'Evenin'!" The scruffy blond man behind the counter chewed on a toothpick and kept one eyeball glued on the small TV set suspended from a ceiling bracket in the corner. On the tube, race cars circled the track. Lap after lap of droning engines blared down from the set.

"Hi," Terra returned his greeting, raising her voice to compete with the roaring television.

"Help ya, ma'am?"

"Actually, I just need directions. And a Coke." She filled a wax cup with ice and pushed the self-serve dispenser lever. "I'm looking for Mrs. Neva Old Elk's place."

He reached one arm up, whacked the TV volume knob with a ruler, and cocked his ear toward her. She repeated her question.

"Ya take Main Street here"—his thumb jerked back toward the two-lane road—"and head up to the fork. Then ya take yer right to the silo then turn right agin' at that big cedar bush. Past that's Neva's place. But she don't like company this time a'night," he added.

"I'm going to see her tomorrow," Terra explained somewhat defensively. "Tonight, I just need to find a motel."

Again, the thumb jerked over his shoulder. "Alita Bear's got a comfy place two blocks down. Ya got yer cable TV and yer queen-sized beds."

At midnight, Terra was still tossing in her queen-sized bed at the Bear's Den. What if this whole trip was a mistake? What if Neva Old Elk slammed the door in her face?

Well, Terra girl, she reasoned, *you can't spend the rest of your life wondering. You've got to know, for better or worse.*

The irony of that phrase was not lost on her as she stared at the knotty pine–paneled ceiling.

The morning sun slanted in the motel room window, bathing the room in yellow brilliance and spreading warmth across Terra's face. She rose quickly, showered, and donned jeans and an MSU sweatshirt. In one quick motion, her hair was twisted up onto the back of her head and pinned.

After checking out of her room, she traversed Staghorn once more, following Main Street to the town's edge. When the road forked, she took the gravel road that aimed at the mountains. She drove until she saw a single silo jutting up on the horizon. Veering to the right again, she bumped over the rutted dirt road until a huge, aged cedar bush loomed in the field. In the distance, a lone chicken hawk circled gracefully in the cloudless blue sky.

Nestled into the hillside straight ahead, a small, tidy farmstead sat at the end of the road. As the truck drew nearer, a border collie bounced enthusiastically from the porch of a small frame house, its tail flicking above its back. It circled the vehicle in a flurry of barking and tail wagging.

"Hi, fella." Terra ruffled the dog's ears as she stepped away from the truck. "Good boy!"

The dog's legs pranced up and down like pistons. Its tail waved even more furiously when Terra spoke. The critter had found an instant friend.

Following the flat rock walkway up to the first step on the porch, Terra noticed two wide-board oak rockers sitting companionably together. At the end of the porch, an old-fashioned swing hung by chains. In front of the wooden-framed screen door, a braided rug encouraged dusty boots to be scraped clean. The whole porch projected an air of comfort, harmony.

Swallowing a little of her fear, Terra reached up and

knocked. The weathered screen door clattered against the door frame with each rap.

Bad idea, bad idea, Terra thought in rhythm with the pounding of her heart as she waited at the unanswered door. *Bad idea, bad idea.*

A noise from within the house grabbed the attention of the tall, thin young woman on the porch. The dog's ears perked up in unison.

Her knees began to shake as Terra narrowed her eyes to see through the dark screen on the door.

It's too late to run away, she realized. *This is it.*

The door creaked open on an aged metal spring. The woman in the doorway moved as though she too were strung with rusting metal. Her movements were slow, measured.

A deeply wrinkled brown hand reached up to discipline a stray silvery lock back into the braid cascading over her shoulder.

The old woman took in every detail of her young caller's face. A wistful smile tugged at the wrinkled flesh of her cheeks but failed to reach her penetrating, weary eyes.

''Are you the girl?'' she asked quietly.

Chapter Seven

She's Terisa's child. Neva knew it immediately. It was there, all right, in the proud way she held her chin, the almost defiant way her eyes took in everything around her.

She was a tall woman, tall for a Crow, with long legs and skinny ankles. Just like Terisa, who always walked fast and could run like the wind. This girl had the same athletic build, narrow-hipped and strong. The same eyes, too, watching everything, shining like polished agate.

She was Terisa's child. Neva felt her mouth tug into a smile, but her heart wouldn't let her eyes smile, too.

"I'm Terra Bartlett," the girl answered. "Are you Neva Old Elk?"

"I am." The woman nodded slowly and stepped back. "Come in."

Terra slipped into a chair near the doorway, her glance around the room registering the Spartan but meticulously clean furnishings. The midmorning sun danced across the wooden floor of the farmhouse.

The parlor itself was an anachronism. No television set stared out at them. No telephone was in evidence. The wood-burning stove dominating one wall was testament to long, cold Montana nights.

An archaic floor lamp stood poised behind a comfortable overstuffed chair in one corner. It was a seating arrangement, Terra realized, that cried out, "Come sit here. Bury your nose in a book. Forget the rest of the world. Just enjoy yourself."

It was a room time had forgotten, a room rich with the patina of age.

The pendulum of an antique clock hanging between long, narrow windows swung patiently, sending its *tick, tick, tick* into the quiet room.

Sitting opposite Terra in a straight-backed armchair, the old woman rested her feet on the edge of an oval braided rug. She wore sturdy shoes, sensible and plain. Above them, the hem of her faded print dress hung unevenly to the middle of cotton-stocking–wrapped legs.

Tick, tick, tick.

Terra's mouth felt full of wool. Her stomach flipped. One hand clutched the other, her thumbnails clicking together nervously. She had to say something, but what?

"This is very awkward for me," she admitted. "I'm not sure what to say."

"You've come for answers." Neva's reply was simple. Her voice held the slight lilt Terra had detected in Whit's words. It was obviously a Crow accent, that melodic softness that slurred consonants just enough to take the harshness out of them and make sentences sound like song. It had fascinated Terra to hear Whit speak; now, she found herself similarly hanging on to each word Neva spoke.

"I have." Terra drew a deep breath and began. "I've come to find out about my birth parents. The court gave me your name as their legal representative. Do you know the woman who gave birth to me?" She cast a beseeching look at the old Indian woman, hoping she would be the source of answers to Terra's questions.

The old woman's fingers traced a rose embroidered on the armchair cover. Strong, unfeminine hands, their movement was incongruously graceful. Her eyes never left the design as she outlined it over and over, nervously.

Her voice was scarcely more than a whisper. "You were born to my daughter, Terisa Old Elk."

"Your daughter?" Digesting the information threatened

to choke the young woman. "So . . . you're . . . you're my grandmother?" she asked, incredulous.

"Yes. I am your grandmother." The woman's hand crept over her lap, her thumbnails scraping against each other nervously.

"Where is my . . ." Terra tried to form the word, finding it impossible. She couldn't say "mother." Nancy Bartlett was her mother.

"Where is," she began again, "your daughter? Where is Terisa Old Elk? Why couldn't she see me instead of letting the court contact you? Is she so ashamed of giving away her baby?"

The words, once started, poured out like water in an unplugged drain. For too long, they had been locked inside her with no one to provide the answers. Now, Terra was helpless to stop the questions from tumbling out.

"Does she ever ask about me? Doesn't she want to see her own daughter? What kind of woman would give up her own baby to complete strangers?"

When Terra's voice cracked with a sob, she lowered her head and swiped at her eyes with the back of her hand. The pent-up frustration was gone, replaced with a quiet desperation to understand the woman who had given her life and then given her away.

In the distance, a bird's trill sliced into the silence, carrying its joyful sound through the screened window into the room. Outside, quaking aspen danced in the faint morning breeze, fragmenting the sunlight into splotches of shadows dancing through the lace curtains.

Terra glared at the old woman.

"And what about my father? Didn't he care either? Where does he fit into this whole thing? Or . . . am I illegitimate?"

"You were born to Terisa Old Elk and her husband, Raymond Light." Neva's fingers continued to outline the cover's embroidery, their movement the only outward sign of nervousness the old woman showed. "The Lights are an honorable Crow family. Your birth brought them great happiness.''

''Until they gave me up,'' Terra interjected angrily. Her emotions were running the gamut from anger to hurt and back again.

''Your parents didn't give you up, girl. It was a choice they couldn't make. They died when you were a week old.''

The words, issued with quiet dignity, struck Terra like a physical blow.

Dead? Since she was a week old?

Now, after all these years of wondering, of resenting, of fearing . . . all these years of not knowing, the answer had been found.

''I . . . didn't know.''

Neva shrugged, shaking her head sadly. ''How could you know?''

''How did they . . . die?'' Deep within her, sympathy for the parents she had never known tempered Terra's words. The anger had subsided, replaced with a deeper emotion.

''They lived up the draw from here.'' Neva nodded toward the window. ''They had a nice farm. Some good horses. We Crows take pride in our horses, you know.'' A hint of a smile crossed Neva's face, as she continued. ''Raymond built a fine house. He had respect, you know, for his wife. He was an honorable man. They brought the baby . . .'' Neva's eyes shone. ''They brought . . . you . . . home to their nice new house. But the wiring in the house wasn't right. Raymond was a proud man, you know, and a good man. Did things on his own, plumbing and such as that. But the wiring was wrong. It was a cold day when they brought you home from the hospital. Raymond, he wanted it warm enough for the baby, you know. He turned the heaters on. But the wiring burned up and started a fire in the walls.''

Neva's voice trembled as she continued, remembering.

''Terisa, she was weak from having her baby. She tried

to get her baby—you—but she fell. There was so much smoke. She couldn't get the baby. She was screaming. Raymond, he was up in the pasture and saw the house on fire. He came running. He couldn't find the baby in the smoke. Both Raymond and Terisa died in the fire.''

The old woman leaned against the chair's backrest, emotionally spent.

Terra's voice was scarcely more than a whisper. ''I'm sorry about your daughter . . .''

Your daughter, she thought. *My birth mother.* It was still almost more than she could comprehend.

''. . . and your son-in-law. It must have been a very painful time for you.''

Neva nodded. Her deeply wrinkled face was a study in serenity as a tentative half-smile washed over her.

The old woman shook her head as if to dismiss her grief. ''This is a time to rejoice. You have come back to me, back to your people. A Crow always comes home.''

Whit's words echoed in Terra's mind: *''A Crow always comes home.''*

How I wish you were here now, Whit! I thought I was stronger than this. I wanted to be detached from it, not get involved. But this woman is my grandmother, Terra agonized. *She's a stranger, but her blood runs in my veins.*

''Was there,'' Terra broached the question timidly, ''ever any chance of keeping me, as a baby? Did I have aunts or uncles to care for me?''

''Terisa was my only child. Raymond had a brother, but he was just a boy then. The Social Services people wouldn't let him raise a baby because of his age. I was alone. My husband died before you were born. After the fire, I got sick and went to the hospital. The people from the agency asked me to give you up. They brought papers while I was in the hospital and took you away.'' The old woman's voice was sadly monotone. ''I thought it was better if the baby . . . if you . . . went with a healthy young couple. They could do more for you than I could. But my heart was sad to give you up. It was a very bad time.''

Raw emotion saturated the old woman's words. She stared out the window. Twenty-seven years had passed since it happened, yet the hurt was as fresh as though it were yesterday. Years of wondering how the child was getting along. Wondering if she had been told she had Crow blood. Hoping somehow, some way, the girl would find her way back to the reservation.

Her eyes returned to the beautiful young woman sitting across the parlor from her. Brown eyes so like Terisa's smiled at her in return.

''I am pleased with you, Terra.'' The remark was like a benediction in the sun-brightened room. ''I think you are a good person.''

''I want to be, Grandmother.'' The word was out before Terra realized she'd said it. *Grandmother.*

The day stole by too quickly, as the two women grew to know each other.

Neva showed Terra the beadwork she had done before age had diminished her eyesight.

''Please, take this sash,'' Neva offered. ''It would be an honor for me if you would accept it.'' The hand-beaded leather sash was a work of art.

''It's beautiful.''

''It was part of Terisa's traditional dance costume. She danced in shawl dances at the Powwow. Terisa was a wonderful dancer,'' she added more for herself than for Terisa's daughter. *It was good,* Neva thought, remembering the times before the fire.

Terra told her grandmother about her work as a game management officer and about her happy life as Nancy and Mason Bartlett's daughter.

They sat on the porch swing and watched the dog chase its tail. Sparrows long accustomed to Neva's handouts gathered near the well pump and pecked at the ground expectantly.

"I need to get a meal put out," Neva stated simply, in the direct, no-nonsense way Terra had come to realize was her grandmother's pattern.

"May I help?"

"There's no need. Everything is ready in the refrigerator. I had a vision last night that a visitor would come today. I hoped it would be you."

The old woman rose from the swing and patted her granddaughter's shoulder.

"Your visit has brought me great joy. It makes my heart soar like an eagle."

Too quickly, the sun faded from the sky. Twilight had draped purple velvet curtains across the foothills.

"I should be going." A glance at her watch told Terra that a three-hour drive from the reservation would put her home after midnight. They had talked together through dinner. There was so much catching up to be done.

"It would please me if you stayed here tonight," Neva offered. The presence of Terisa's daughter had brought joy into the house; the girl's laughter rippled like happy rainwater.

Terra's arms encircled the old woman's shoulders. "It would please me as well, Grandmother."

"Will you honor me by learning the Crow word for grandmother?" Neva's eyes caught Terra's and held. It was a big step, having the girl accept the Crow ways. Perhaps, bit by bit, Neva thought, she could introduce Terisa's daughter to the ways of her people. It was worth the chance.

Terra nodded. "Tell me."

"You would say Kaalá," Neva explained. "It is the traditional Crow way for a girl to address her grandmother."

"Kaalá," Terra repeated. The inflection in her tone did not match the lyrical rolling sound Neva gave the word. Still, she was pleased to learn it.

Kaalá. It was what Whit's sisters would call their grand-mother, too. Terra remembered Whit explaining how each of the children in his family had learned at least a few words of the Crow language. It was important to him to retain his tribe's culture. She recalled the love in his satin-smooth voice when he talked about his family and their reservation home.

Terra blinked, trying to dispel the memory of his smile. *Will I ever stop missing you, Whit? Will the pain in my heart ever go away?*

It was after midnight when Terra awoke with a start. In the pitch black of Neva's parlor, where the young woman had bedded down on the sofa, the silence was broken by a soft lowing. She listened intently. It came from the front porch.

Terra rose quietly, pulling her sweatshirt sleeves down to ward off the cool night air. Opening the front door a crack, she strained to hear.

The sound came again.

She opened the door farther and looked out into the moonlit night. As her eyes adjusted to the darkness on the porch, she detected a figure.

"Grandmother? Kaalá?"

"Yes," Neva answered softly. "Come out and enjoy the moon." The old woman stood on the porch, gazing across the foothills. Wrapped in a quilt, with her thick hair in a single braid down her back, her dignity persevered. Her face, in the light of the moon, was peaceful.

How, Terra wondered, could she not love this woman, this ancestor of hers, this noble, dear old woman!

"I thought I heard singing." Terra rubbed her eyes and stepped through the open screen door. The border collie's tail thumped a welcome on the wooden porch floor as the two women stood in the moonlight.

Neva chuckled. "I was praying. Sometimes I forget I am not a coyote or a wolf. I am only their sister, but I bay at the moon much as they do. They call it singing. I call it praying. It is the night of a warm moon and I am thankful to the Great Spirit for bringing you back to your people.''

The air was fragrant with the scent of sagebrush pervading the night. Reflecting off mineral-laden rocks in the far hills, the moonlight was like molten gold.

''Kaalá?''

''Yes?''

''Would you . . . would you say a prayer for the woman who gave me life? And for her husband, too?'' She tried to bring herself to call them her parents. But it was too new, too raw an emotion. Nancy and Mason Bartlett were her parents. It would take time, both women knew. Still, something more than mere curiosity over the complexity of her past created an urgency in Terra to acknowledge the Crow couple.

''I will do that,'' the old woman responded, her voice husky with emotion. ''Tomorrow, if you like, we'll visit their graves and you can pay your respects.''

Seeing her birth parents' graves the next afternoon evoked more emotion in Terra than she was prepared to face. She touched their headstones reverently, outlining the dates on the stones slowly with her fingertip.

The hurt and fear had dissipated after Neva had told her the circumstances of her adoption. Now, seeing the final resting place of Terisa and Raymond, seeing their names carved in stone, Terra realized she was all that remained on Earth of the two people. Even her name, she knew now, was a contraction of their names. Terisa. Raymond. Terra.

''I'm glad my name wasn't changed when I was adopted.'' Her confession surprised her. Twenty-four hours ago, she had no feelings but scorn for the woman who had given birth to her. Now, having heard the circumstances surrounding her adoption, her understanding allowed her to exercise the compassion she felt.

Neva nodded. "It speaks of the bond between your parents."

On Sunday, both women talked at once sometimes; there was so much to learn about each other. The old woman and the young one stole glances back and forth, watching for similarities in their motions, their laugh, their eyes. And finding those points where one mirrored the other brought them even closer together.

Sitting in the shade of massive cottonwood trees in Neva's backyard, they caught up on twenty-seven years of news about each other's life.

"Several months ago," Neva said at one point, "an elk came to me in a dream. He told me he had seen Terisa's daughter in the mountains where the great elk herds winter. I was glad to hear about you."

Several months ago, Terra realized, she had been collaring elk at Hannon Pass. The coincidence was unsettling. Dreams and visions, Terra recalled, were part of traditional Indian culture. That, she remembered from a Native American studies class in college. But this was real. This was her life, invading someone's dreams.

Yes, it was unsettling, to say the least.

Neva wove white hollyhock blossoms into a chain and draped it over Terra's head.

"You look like a bride." The old woman's laugh crinkled her eyes.

"Not much chance of that." Terra readjusted the flowers over her shoulders. Her softly spoken comment held a cynical edge not lost on Neva.

"Do you have a man?" Neva's eyes were bright and disarmingly direct.

I had a man, Terra nearly answered.

I could have had a man, she corrected herself.

I wish I had that man, she agonized silently.

"No, Kaalá. Not anymore."

"Why?"

"We," Terra began, "we, uh, couldn't agree on things."

The grunt Neva emitted, coupled with her sideways glance of derision, made Terra laugh in spite of herself.

"What does that look mean?"

Neva shook her head slowly. "Men and women don't have to agree on things. Where there is respect, where there is honor and love, there needn't always be agreement."

"He's a Crow," Terra offered by way of explanation.

It didn't explain anything to Neva. "So are you, child."

"Our ways seemed too different. He was raised on the reservation. Whitman Bull Chief. Maybe you know his family, the Bull Chief family from Blue Rock?"

Neva nodded. "Oh, yes, Bull Chiefs. I know their family clan. Yes. They're a good family. Respected on the reservation. Whitman has three sisters. They want him to get married and have children. He's a good man. He comes home to visit frequently."

"He asked me to come here with him. I wouldn't do it. I was too angry and too fearful."

"Fearful?"

"Of finding out why I was given up for adoption. I didn't know. Somehow, I thought something was wrong with me that my parents—my birth parents—wouldn't keep me."

"And yet you are here now. That must please him."

Terra squinted into the distance. "He doesn't know I'm here. I did this for me, Kaalá, not for him."

A smile folded Neva's sun-weathered skin and danced in her eyes. "When you love a man, what you have done for yourself, you have done for him."

After dinner, with a promise she would return in August for the Crow Fair, Terra stowed her bag behind her truck seat and said her good-byes to her grandmother.

"I don't know how to express what I'm feeling, Kaalá. Thank you for everything you've given me." She pulled the old woman to her and held her tightly, relishing the comfortable, loving feeling Neva exuded. "I'll write to you, often."

"I'll see you in August." Neva smiled and stepped back as Terra opened the truck door and slid inside. "You will come back again, won't you?" The old woman's eyebrows knit in concern.

"Of course," Terra answered, grinning. "A Crow always comes home."

She depressed the clutch and turned the key in the ignition.

Click.

Terra tried the starter again.

Click.

"Dead battery?" Neva cocked her head and watched as Terra turned the key again.

"It's the starter." Disgusted with herself for deferring maintenance on the truck, Terra recognized the problem immediately. Frustration clouded her face. "It's been going out for a month and I just put off taking it to the garage."

"You can stay over," Neva offered.

"I have to be at work by seven in the morning. We've got game tracking and I have to be there." She opened the truck door and stepped out. "There isn't a garage around here, is there?"

"Nothing open tonight. In Lame Deer, there's a shop that'll be open tomorrow. But," Neva added, "Raymond's brother lives over the hill. Let's walk over. He can give you a ride back."

"It's almost a three-hour drive. I can't ask him to drive me all that way, then have to turn around and drive back here to the reservation tonight."

"Of course you can ask it," Neva said nonchalantly. "You're family."

As they left the graveled road and started west on the interstate, Terra glanced across the seat of the low-slung sports car at Raymond's brother.

At her uncle, she corrected herself. Forty-eight hours ago, she didn't know she had a grandmother or an uncle. Now, she had begun learning the Crow ways from Neva, and was zooming down the highway in the dark with her uncle, Alexx Light.

"This is quite a car." Accustomed to her aging pickup truck with its inherent bumps and squeaks, Terra found the luxurious sports car heavenly.

"We Crows are known for our love of horses. I just prefer mine under the hood," Alexx joked.

Terra noted her uncle's superbly tailored suit and hand-made western boots. This man was accustomed to the best, she realized. He surrounded himself with fine things.

Neva had told her, on their walk to Alexx's house, of his achievements as a building contractor. Both of the Light boys, both Raymond and Alexx, were good builders, Neva pointed out.

"You're obviously a very successful businessman," she observed.

"Success," Alexx answered, "only means I've been able to construct buildings to help my people. Schools and hospitals."

"I passed the new hospital on my way across the reservation. It's beautiful. I like how you incorporated Crow symbols in the brickwork trim. I'd say it's a work of art."

"I'm one of those lucky people who gets paid for doing something truly enjoyable."

"That's how I feel about my job," Terra responded. "But working for the state government, I'll never make the kind of money you're making."

"Prosperity doesn't have anything to do with money, girl." Alexx's eyes scanned the highway while he addressed her remark. "True prosperity is having the love of a family surrounding you."

"Does it seem as strange to you as it does to me to discover you have a niece?"

Terra's openness surprised and pleased him. She had her father's directness and her mother's beauty.

"I remember when the old woman told me you were gone." Alexx's reference to Neva was one of respect. In the Native-American culture, Terra knew, acknowledging someone as "old" was an expression of admiration. Tribal elders were treated with great reverence. "It made her very, very sad. I was just a kid myself, sixteen years old. Our parents were dead and I had been staying with a family in town until I finished high school and could move in with Raymond and Terisa. The day you left our family, I wanted to run after the people from Social Services and pull you out of their car. It was crazy, I know. Here I was, a skinny kid of sixteen, shouting that I could raise a baby."

"I'm sorry for all the hurt you've been through."

"When they took you away"—Alexx's voice was barely above a whisper—"they took away the last blood of my family."

Terra nodded in commiseration. "It must've been heartbreaking for both you and Neva."

Alexx watched the white line on the highway, reflecting in the headlights of his car as it purred through the darkness.

"As much as I grieved, I know it was worse for her. She was badly burned in the fire and while she was in the hospital, she had to relive the trauma of the fire and of losing her daughter. Then, she lost her granddaughter as well."

"Neva was in the fire?" Horror widened Terra's eyes.

The faint light of the dashboard cast a subtle glow across the chiseled planes of her uncle's face. He glanced briefly at Terra before returning his gaze to the highway.

"Of course you wouldn't know," Alexx realized aloud. "Neva went to stay with them, to care for you and your mother, when Terisa brought you home from the hospital. She was there that night. It was Neva who pulled you out of the burning house."

"She didn't tell me."

"She wouldn't." Her uncle delivered the remark with a sense of acceptance. "Cold moon honor, you know."

"I'm afraid," Terra confessed, "I don't know what that means."

Alexx glanced in the rearview mirror, then flicked on his right turn indicator. The high-performance sports car decelerated as he pulled off the highway, coasting to a complete stop. Shutting off the motor, he opened his door and motioned for Terra to do the same.

Both stepped out into the cool night and walked to the shoulder of the road. It was nearly midnight, and the highway was deserted. Crickets and night birds had begun their nocturnal serenade. Pine-scented air encircled them. It was exhilarating to the point of being almost magical.

"Do you see what the warm moon does to the land?" Alexx motioned to the huge golden ball suspended in the black sky.

"It brightens the countryside like day," his niece observed.

"Exactly." Alexx walked to the edge of the meadow and stood with his upturned face in the moonlight. "When the moon is full, what we call a warm moon, deeds are readily seen. It is easy to do the right thing—the honorable thing—when everyone can see you. But when a deed is done on the cold moon, under the cover of darkness, no one sees it. Deeds performed under the cold moon live within the heart. They are the deepest goodness, the most noble deeds. Doing something good without the expectation of recognition or reward is known as cold moon honor."

"Neva saved me," Terra murmured, "and never expected to be thanked."

"And then," Alexx added, "she was willing to give you to people who could better care for you than she could. Her love for you was that great."

"I don't doubt that love now. I used to." It was hard for Terra to admit it, even to herself. "How unselfish she was, to give up part of her daughter, part of herself. It would be a huge sacrifice.''

Alexx turned and rounded in front of the car. He glanced over his shoulder once again at the full moon.

''Never forget the honor she bestowed on you, Terra.''

The remainder of the drive was entertaining. Alexx recalled stories of her father's youth: Raymond's fishing escapades, his homemade raft, his mongrel dog appropriately named Stainer.

He talked about Terisa, and how he had adored her with the unabashed puppy love only a sixteen-year-old boy can experience.

''She was lovely. And smart. Their house was filled with her handiwork. She sewed curtains for the windows. And could she cook! Raymond was lucky to find such a good woman.''

''What about you, Uncle?'' Terra directed her question at Alexx with complete candor. ''Were you ever married? Or is that beautiful house of yours off-limits to women?'' Terra recalled the huge, beautifully rustic stone-and-wood showplace situated on a hillside near Neva's house.

''I never wanted to devote the time to a wife that I did to my business,'' Alexx answered honestly, ''until last year when I met the woman of my dreams.''

''Do tell.''

''Her name is Miranda Tall Bear. She's back East finishing her master's degree in environmental law. When she returns to the reservation, we'll get married.''

Terra was pleased. It hadn't taken her long to recognize Alexx Light as a hardworking, caring man. ''Good for you.''

''Well, my friends are still amazed that after all these years of being single, I've finally fallen deeply and irrevocably in love.'' Alexx chuckled at himself.

I know the feeling, Terra admitted only to herself. She had been able to turn around and walk away from every man she'd ever met.

Until Whit.

With him, she'd worn her heart on her sleeve. Now, that heart was in pieces, and one piece was clear across the country.

It was nearly one in the morning when they reached Terra's condo. Alexx walked her to the door, carrying her bag for her.

"You should come in, Uncle Alexx. At least have a cup of coffee before you start back." Terra unlocked the condo door and snapped on the porch light.

"No. It'll keep me awake on the highway," he joked. "You need to get to bed. Tomorrow's a work day for you. Being my own boss has its advantages. I can show up late for work! Besides, it's been a pretty exciting weekend, hasn't it? For both of us, discovering each other again. Just think: the last time I saw you, you were only nine days old. Believe me, I'm not going to let you only come back into our family every twenty-seven years! You're part of us forever."

"I'll be back next weekend to get my truck. I'm sure my friend Pam can drive me down."

"Are you sure? I can come get you."

"No, I'll get there. Thanks. And besides, I'm coming next month for the Crow Fair. I promised Grandmother."

"I'll see you then, little one."

"Thanks, Uncle Alexx." Terra stood in the triangle of illumination from the porch light and stretched on her tip-toes to embrace the tall man before her. "Thank you for telling me about my parents."

"Take care of yourself. And remember us." Alexx grinned at her, and she saw a resemblance between his smile and her own.

He turned and bounced down the stairs with the vigor of a man much younger than his forty-three years. He was happy. Being with Terra meant being with a part of his beloved brother again.

* * *

Whitman Bull Chief had fought the feelings that kept him in Montana two days longer than his business dictated. It was time, he realized, to talk to Terra. Time to assure her that no matter how she felt about staying away from the reservation, he would respect her wishes. He had been wrong, he knew, to impose his rules on their relationship.

If she couldn't get past her adoption, he'd be more sensitive to her feelings. Whatever it took to get them back together, he was willing to accede. The time they'd been apart only proved to him how much he needed her in his life again.

All weekend long, from Friday night until half an hour ago, he'd called the condo. Her answering machine greeted him with its standard message, giving no clue as to her whereabouts. His last call had been at midnight. She had to work tomorrow. Where was she?

He left the motel and steered his rental car down Boulder Avenue toward her condo. Maybe she had just gotten home. Maybe her answering machine was jammed, and she hadn't gotten his message saying he wanted to see her. He couldn't tell an answering machine how much he loved her and needed her. That, he wanted to tell her in person.

He rounded the corner to her street and turned into the courtyard fronting her condominium complex.

It was only then he saw the sleek sports car at the curb. His eyes followed the sidewalk up to her door, where the golden porch light revealed Terra embracing a tall, dark-haired man.

Whit hit the brakes and stopped short of the path of light shining from the doorway. He watched with agonizing clarity as the couple on the porch parted and Terra's smile followed the man down the sidewalk. The stranger folded his lanky body into the expensive, showy car and honked as he pulled away from the curb.

"It didn't take you long to replace me in your life, Terra," Whit mumbled to himself in disbelief as he watched her eyes follow the sports car until it turned out of sight.

The young woman went inside, completely unaware of Whit's presence beyond the hedge. She snapped the porch light off, leaving only the moonlight to illuminate the courtyard.

Chapter Eight

August's unrelenting sun and eighty-degree days were welcomed by residents who joked that Montana had only two seasons: this winter and next winter.

On Zuercher Lake, sailboats painted multihued slashes against the clear blue sky. The same lake that provided prolific ice fishing five months of the year now was peppered with fishing enthusiasts and water-skiers.

Pam Craft gazed longingly at the lake as they passed the turnoff.

"You know, if we won the state lottery, we could quit our jobs and be over there right now, waterskiing and drinking ice-cold lemonade instead of sweltering in this truck."

"Then who," Terra challenged her coworker, "would do our range surveys and monitor the mule deer population?"

"Let the mule deer join us at the lake. We'll train them to water-ski." Pam grinned like a leprechaun. "I know I'd sure rather be at the lake today than tracking deer in this heat."

"This is our last day in the field. Tomorrow, we can get back to our nice un-air-conditioned offices," Terra reminded her jokingly.

Dust, like the ghost of a vehicle that had stirred it up some time before, hung above the turnoff road. Deerflies droned in the white-hot sunlight as vegetation hung limply awaiting sundown's cooling respite.

"The last time I was past this road was the night we were all at the club for Open Microphone Night. I stopped on the way home just to enjoy the stars."

Pam did a double take. "Alone?"

"Alone. But actually, I guess I wasn't completely alone after all. I saw some lights over there past that grove." She pointed to the wooded draw across from the road.

Pam glanced at the spot. "It's pretty isolated further up here off the road. Don't you stop here alone at night. It isn't safe."

Parking the truck, Terra consulted her notebook. "That's where I'm getting a radio signal from One fifty point six." She referred to the mule deer by its radio collar's frequency. "It's been steady from this same spot for two days now. I'm wondering if he's wounded or if he's just lost his collar. Let's walk down into the gulch and see if we can spot it."

Her colleague nodded. "I'll radio the office to confirm our location, and let them know we'll be doing ground surveys in the area all afternoon."

"Would you please grab that canteen, too, Pam? We've got acres to cover today." Slipping her notebook into her backpack, she hoisted the bag across her shoulder blades and buckled it in place. Her hand-held receiver and antennae were bleating the static which would change to telltale beeps when a deer's signal transmitted.

The first mile went quickly, as they followed the road partway before angling off through the trees. The signal had come from this area, and they looked for either an injured deer or its shed collar.

"He could be anywhere in this area," Terra muttered as much to herself as to her coworker as they scoured the area. The drying grass crunched underfoot as they slid down a dusty embankment and followed a game trail into a thicket.

The radio signal strengthened as they neared the woods. The transmitter was nearby.

"Here it is!"

Pam hopped through the brush and retrieved the radio collar lying abandoned on a fallen tree trunk. The deer had marked the tree trunk. Obviously, it was during the ritual marking that the collar had worked off. The mule deer was nowhere in sight.

They checked the collar's markings: Montana Department of Fish, Wildlife & Parks, Number 150.6.

Depositing the collar in Terra's bag, Pam took off her billed cap and wiped her forehead.

"Gosh, it's hot today!"

"It should cool off pretty soon." Terra looked at her watch. It was nearly five. They'd hiked all afternoon.

Windmere Meadow, carpeted in a rainbow of native wildflowers, stretched out before them as the two women hiked over the pass and started into the Madison River drainage.

Continuing the mule deer survey, Terra checked the receiver while Pam read off the list of collar frequencies one by one.

"One fifty point eight."

"One fifty point nine."

The numbers kept coming as they trudged through the underbrush.

"One fifty-one point one."

"One fifty-one point two."

They watched for tracks. Their eyes, accustomed to finding telltale markings on low-growing tree limbs, squinted against the sun and scanned the fields.

A second mortality signal had come in last week from this area. As they approached a draw, the signal doubled in speed and intensity.

"Let's look by the riverbank," Terra suggested, knowing wolves and mountain lions often followed the river.

"There it is!" She bolted, clutching the receiver as she jogged through the tall grass.

At the same time, Pam spotted the mule deer carcass in the path ahead.

"Well." Terra sighed deeply. "It looks like we've got a mountain lion kill."

Pam nodded. The lion had partially devoured the deer, then loosely covered the carcass with scratched-back dirt and pine needles.

The deer's radio collar lay a short distance from the site, transmitting a mortality signal.

"An efficient, natural kill," Terra commented. Mountain lions stalked their prey, ambushed them, then bulldogged them down for a quick kill. It was part of the cycle of nature.

"I was afraid when we got the mortality signal it was poachers. I haven't forgotten the wolf we found here in January."

The two women set about recording the necessary data, then added the radio collar to Terra's pack.

"Shall we call it a day?" Pam squinted at the skyline. Dusk was not far off, and they were miles from the main road.

Terra nodded in agreement. "Let's follow the logging road down."

There was no darkness like that which fell in the mountains on a starless night. The blackness that enveloped them was absolute, with a dense cloud cover obscuring the moon.

"We should've started back a little earlier." Pam's remark was such a gross understatement that both women began to laugh. It was ludicrous.

"I can't believe it's so warm and humid tonight," Pam commented in the darkness. "It's like walking in a dog's mouth."

"Tell the dog to open his mouth," Terra responded with a giggle, "so we can see where we're going."

That they were familiar with the road was their saving grace. Their sense of direction was faultless. At last, they reached the end of the logging road. Their truck was less than a mile away.

A glimmer of light, faint and fleeting, flickered in Terra's peripheral vision.

"Did you see that light?"

Pam's voice came out of the stygian night. "Where?"

Terra realized the futility of pointing in the dark. "It's moving over there, at about two o'clock."

Pam's eyes followed the direction. "What is it?"

"Looks like somebody's got a lantern. But this is pretty far from a campground. Maybe we should check it out."

They forged through knee-deep grass in the dark, snagging an occasional fallen tree limb in their path. The light remained steady as they drew closer.

Within the perimeter of the light halo thrown by the powerful halogen lantern stood two figures. The door of their ramshackle cabin gaped open. Fluttering moths punctuated the glare pouring from within.

"Well, well," a raspy voice croaked as Terra and Pam stepped into the circle of light. "What do we have here? You gals out snoopin' around in the dark?"

In the uneven light from the cabin door, the man's corpulent face was shadowed and sinister. He stepped forward, frowning from one woman to the other. The odor of grease, perspiration, and human filth hung on him like a cloak.

"What're ya doin' here?" he snarled. His companion lurked in the background. He reminded Terra of a dog in a dump as he paced menacingly, watching them with suspicion.

"We're with the Fish, Wildlife & Parks Service." Terra found her voice. "We've been tracking mule deer this afternoon. We're on our way back to our truck."

"You got a gun, girlie?" A sneer creeping over the man's features was directed at Terra. From where he stood, the smell of his breath permeated the air.

"We're not armed. We're in game management, not enforcement."

Both women stood rigidly still. The tension in the air was palpable.

"You sure you wasn't snoopin' around here?" He stepped closer.

Despite being nearly disabled by his stench, Terra bristled. "Look here. We've got a job to do. Whatever you *men,*" she emphasized the word sarcastically, "are doing is your business. We're going to our truck."

The second man, a scrawny scarecrow with a greasy baseball cap topping straggly hair, stepped forward. Addressing his cohort, his eyes shifted nervously between the two women.

"They's spyin' on us, Leon. Them government trucks have been runnin' up and down the road for months. They's spyin' on us."

"Shut up, Fred," the intensely odiferous man squawked. "I'll handle this."

His hand shot out and grabbed Terra's forearm.

Instinctively, she recoiled, shaking loose from his grasp. Again, his hand snaked out. He grabbed her arm and held on. She could see the grease under his fingernails, and it sent a shudder through her.

"Keep your filthy hands off her!" Pam leaped forward, throwing him off balance as she landed full force against him.

The man's grotesquely obese body hit the ground with a resounding thump. Pam fell on top of him, then quickly rolled to her knees and stood up.

"Are you okay?" Terra reached to dust off pine needles sticking to Pam's arms.

"I'm all right." Her voice was tight, her jaw rigid. Pam was mad all over now. "But if he thinks he can put his filthy paws on us, I'll . . ."

Click.

The women turned in unison, and looked down the barrel of a pistol, cocked to fire.

The scarecrow lookalike inched closer to them, brandishing the weapon like a mad orchestra conductor wildly gesturing with a chrome-plated baton.

Terra's heart began a drumbeat in her throat. Her tongue had turned cottony and darted nervously across her dry lips. At her side, Pam was shaking. Her upper arm, trembling violently, quaked against Terra's.

"We're okay, Pam." She spoke with exaggerated calmness. *Let them think they're in control,* she told herself. Her eyes were riveted to the long-barreled pistol. "These men don't want any trouble."

"You girls come with me." With a wave of the gun, the man motioned toward the cabin. "You're gonna have to stay here till we decide what we're gonna do with you."

Single file, they walked toward the cabin. The rickety, splintered stairs groaned under the weight of their footsteps. Near the doorway, the smell of solvents and grease prickled Terra's nostrils.

Dominating the far end of the cabin was a closed garage door, its panels decrepit and peeling. Inside the structure, a blue Buick sat with the hood yawning open like a patient awaiting dental work.

Workbenches laden with engine parts ran the length of the cabin. Rollered tool chests sat with drawers hanging open, exposing an assortment of wrenches, socket sets, and pliers.

"Get that there rope, Fred. We'll tie these girlies up for now."

With a length of clothesline rope dangling from one bony hand and the gun in the other, Fred approached the women.

"Git in the corner, Blondie," he snarled at Pam. Nodding toward the wall, his baseball cap flew off, sending his hair fanning out like a rooster's comb. "And don't rile me, unless you feel lucky."

He was trying his darnedest, the women realized, to imitate Clint Eastwood. It was a futile attempt.

"Take that backpack off," he ordered Terra. "Put yer hands together."

Both women complied. He bound Terra's wrists and ankles, then turned to Pam and extended the rope to her clenched hands. Roughly, he encircled her legs and wrists with the remaining length of rope and pulled it taut.

"Come on, Fred," his swinelike companion bellowed, "we gotta get to town and make a delivery. Them fellas ain't gonna wait all night for us." With a broad swipe of his fat arm, he gestured at the women. "They ain't goin' nowheres. Come on. Now!"

Leon hitched his grease-stiffened jeans to a point somewhere around his immense overhanging belly, and glared at no one in particular. Sweat ringed the underarms of his grimy shirt and beaded on his unshaven upper lip.

He was nervous. That much was obvious. Things hadn't gone the way he had planned.

"Hold yer horses, Leon, I'm coming." Fred backed away from his captives. His eyes scanned the corner where the women were hitched together. "Don't try no funny business while we're gone," he threatened. He narrowed his eyes, just like he'd seen tough guys do in the movies.

The unkempt twosome stomped down the cabin steps. Revving the engine of their pickup, they showered pebbles and dirt against the front of the cabin as the truck peeled out and disappeared into the night.

With the lanterns out, the cabin was plunged into total darkness. The unclean odor of the men remained, mingling with the oil and gasoline smell of car parts.

For a moment, neither woman spoke.

Then Pam groaned. "What have we gotten into, Terra? Who are these jokers, anyway?"

"Two men," Terra said with a shudder, "with the world's worst grammar and an abhorrence of deodorant."

"Ha ha ha," Pam emphasized each syllable. "What are they doing that's so secretive?"

"Didn't you notice this place when they brought us in here?" Terra answered over her shoulder. "It's a chop shop."

"Then why don't I smell broiled pork?"

"Ha ha ha," Terra reciprocated. "Not that kind of chop.

Chop, as in dismantling cars and selling them piece by piece. All the parts on those tables''—she nodded toward the center of the cabin—''couldn't have come from that one Buick. There are hundreds of car parts here. My guess is, they're stripping parts from stolen cars and fencing them. This close to the Canadian border, they're probably sending them out of the country, too. It's a lucrative business and less chancy than selling the stolen vehicle in one whole piece.''

''So they probably made a run with parts tonight?''

''That's my guess.''

''You think they'll be gone until morning?''

Terra shrugged, to the extent her bound hands and feet would allow movement. ''It's hard to say.''

''Terra?''

''Yah, Pam?''

''We've got to get out of here.''

''I know. They know we'll have the sheriff here if we get away. When those two goons get back, they'll make certain we can't cause them any more trouble. If we hadn't stumbled on this camp, they'd be in the clear.''

Pam's sigh was ragged. ''I don't know about you, but I can't move. Fred, the toothless wonder, bound me pretty tightly.''

Terra felt Pam's deep breaths as they sat back to back. ''I feel like suing my legs for custody of my feet. They don't seem to even belong to me anymore. This rope's cutting off circulation.''

The cabin groaned with each breeze, popping and cracking. Outside, crickets rubbed a rhapsody in the darkness. Occasionally, an owl hooted.

Squirming to shift into a more comfortable position, Pam worked one hand down to the side, pulling the rope more tightly across her back.

''Well, at least I can see my wristwatch now. Thank goodness for lighted watch dials!'' Her attempt at humor was feeble. ''It's almost midnight.''

The floor was hard and cold. Seeping through the crack beneath the cabin door, the nippy mountain air crawled across the wooden floor like a hairy-legged spider and crept up over the women, chilling them to the bone.

It seemed to Terra that days had gone by before Pam announced, "It's almost two."

No position afforded any comfort. Cramps in their legs were replaced by numbness and its resulting chill in their feet. Terra began to shiver, her shoulder blades knocking against her friend.

"I've never been so cold." Pam's remark was uttered through chattering teeth. "Good old Montana summers: sweltering during the day and freezing at night!"

"Think of the warmest thing you can," Terra suggested. "Maybe you can will yourself into being warm."

"Listen, buddy," Pam was resolute, "if I thought I could attain something through sheer will, I'd will a pillow underneath me. This floor is harder than a brick. Every bone in my legs is trying to poke through the skin. No, better yet, I'd will myself into the hot tub at my apartment, with a cup of hot cocoa in my hand!"

"Go for it, girl," Terra teased. As long as she kept Pam occupied by talking, they didn't seem to notice the cold as badly.

Pam leaned back, savoring the warmth of Terra's back as they remained bound together. *Funny,* she thought, *I've always leaned on Terra. Now I'm literally doing just that.*

"Terra?"

"Hmmm?"

"If you thought you were going to die, what would you change in your life?"

"Listen to me, Pam, we're going to get out of this mess. So don't you go talking about dying."

In the darkness, Pam snorted contemptuously. "I don't mean like in die right now. I'm saying, what would you change about your life if you could?"

"From this point on?"

"Yeah."

"Ah, the nagging perplexities of life." Terra's laugh bordered on irony. "I'd be nicer to people."

"Terra Bartlett." Pam's words were harsh. "Cut it out. You couldn't be any nicer."

"More compassionate? More caring?"

"Maybe," Pam agreed. "We all could. I'd be nicer, too. And I'd buy blue contact lenses."

Terra scooted one leg under the other. Her back felt miserably cramped. "I'd tell my mom and dad more often just how much I love them. Heck, I'd tell everybody how much I love them. Nobody'd ever have to wonder if they were loved as long as I'm around."

Pam laughed out loud. "So you'd run around telling everybody how much they mean to you?"

"Yep, starting with you, girl. You're the best. Thanks for being my friend."

"Easy enough," Pam commented drolly.

"And I'd travel to Russia and see all the places I've read about. But I'd go in the summer. I never want to be cold again."

"Wouldn't it be nice if you had Whit Bull Chief here to keep you warm?" Pam mused.

Even in the dark, Pam knew Terra was smiling.

"I can't think of anything nicer," her friend admitted. "I've missed him terribly."

"Do you think you two will get back together?"

"I'm going to work on it, Pam. I know that now. When I was being pigheaded, I expected him to read my mind."

"And he couldn't?"

"You know . . ." Terra's voice in the darkness was pensive. ". . . I think the poor guy really tried. I thought he was being unreasonable in wanting me to go to the reservation, but now I realize he had my best interests at heart. He knew I would never fully accept myself until I confronted my past."

"Sounds like you've done some serious thinking on

things.'' Pam had noticed a certain serenity in Terra that hadn't been there before her visit to the Indian reservation. It was a sense of peace that carried over into everything Terra did.

''My grandmother is a wise woman.'' Terra's voice was filled with reverence. ''She made me realize the bitterness I've carried all these years. I guess I felt nobody could ever love me because my biological parents had given me up for adoption. Now I see how goofy I was to feel that way. If Whit will just forgive me for being so stupid, I know we can be happy together.''

In the years she and Terra had worked together, Pam never heard Terra talk so openly about her feelings. It was a good sign. Terra was on the right road to happiness.

Or would be, Pam corrected herself, if they could just get out of this mess.

''All we need now is to get out of here.''

A note of desperation crept into Terra's voice as she responded. ''Tied up like a couple of pigs at a barbecue, we're stuck in this cabin until those jerks come back.''

An idea, as bright as a beacon shining through the darkness, came to Pam.

''Can you move your leg toward me?''

''What?''

''Move your leg back. There'll be some slack in the rope around my arm if you move your leg.''

''And the reason would be . . . ?''

''You'll see.'' Pam's voice was laced with confidence.

''Not in this pitch black, I won't,'' Terra joked.

''I just thought of something I started collecting.'' Pam's response was enigmatic.

''Which collection—the railroad stuff, the snowglobes, the coffee mugs with pictures of Elvis, or the doorknobs?''

''None of those. Move your leg.''

Terra complied. Pushing her leg toward Pam, she felt the rope tighten as Pam's wrist twisted and slipped free. As quickly as she withdrew it from the rope, Pam moved her hand down to pull up the hem of her uniform pants.

Terra recognized the urgency of Pam's actions.

"You've got a plan, don't you?"

"More than a plan." Pam huffed as she maneuvered her pantleg past the confining rope and reached into her boot top. "I've got a knife."

"A knife?"

"A knife."

"You carry a knife in your boot?" Terra was incredulous. "Who the heck do you think you are, Pam, Crocodile Dundee?"

"Funny. I'm rescuing you and you're making fun of me. Well, it so happens"—she sighed with mock self-importance, then laughed—"I started a knife collection for my brother. I bought this one at a flea market last weekend. But then I decided to keep it. It has all sorts of gadgets on it, and it looked like something that might come in handy when we're in the woods. Remember when we ran into the deer that had gotten stuck in baling twine? A knife would've come in handy. So anyway, I stuck it in my boot this morning and forgot about it until just now."

"I'm never going to complain about your collections again." Terra's promise was heartfelt. "Can you cut us loose?"

"I can try. But I can't move my hands much with this rope on. Maybe I can saw through down by my ankles and pull loose from there."

Tugging and pulling, Pam held the knife to her mouth and opened the blade with her teeth. No symphony was sweeter than the click as the blade locked into place.

"Bend backward as far as you can," Pam instructed. "I'll need the slack in the rope to pull away as I cut."

In the darkness, Terra heard and felt, rather than saw, the blade slicing through the rope. Both women rocked as the blade sawed back and forth.

The gentle release of pressure on Terra's leg signaled Pam's success. The rope was cut.

"You did it!"

"Here. Help me get this rope off."

They yanked and jerked, stepping out of the confining ties. Disoriented in the cabin's murky shadows, they bumped into tables stacked with auto parts.

Something fell to the floor with a dull thud, echoing throughout the structure.

"Let's get out of here." Relief lightened Terra's voice. "It'll be light soon and we can get to the truck before those stooges get back here. Then we can radio the sheriff's office."

She felt around in the fleeting darkness before dawn, found her backpack slouched in the corner where she had dropped it, and shrugged it on.

"Ready?" She could barely see Pam's outline.

"Boy, am I ready!"

Terra felt for the crude wire door handle and yanked hard. The door swung open with a screech. Two sets of footsteps thudded down the rickety stairs as the women descended from the cabin and crossed the clearing.

The stars seemed to brighten the night, after the pitch black of the cabin's interior.

"Listen!" Pam's voice was hushed with anxiety.

Both women strained to hear what they hoped they were not hearing.

Headlights flickered as they beamed between the trees and bounced over the bumpy forest floor. Gears ground in protest as the truck scrunched across the rocky path and rolled to a stop in front of the cabin.

"Run, Pam!" Terra heard herself scream.

Chapter Nine

Pam dodged to her left, escaping the glare of the truck's headlights. Beyond the perimeter of their luminescence, the forest was a study of murky shadows in the predawn hours. The darkness engulfed everything with its black-silhouetted trees and shrouded trails. Progress on the path was accomplished more by sound than by sight, as Pam's footsteps told in snapping twigs and crunching rocks. Her labored breathing hissed through the darkness as she ran.

Terra followed, halfway pushing her friend ahead as their slovenly captors jumped from the truck and pursued the women.

Terra's arms flew forward defensively. Branches and brush clutched at her clothing and snagged her hair. Her shirtsleeve caught on a branch. Pulling it loose, she winced as the bough whipped back and snapped across her arm. There was no time to let the pain register: they had to reach the truck.

Completely disoriented by their flight in the darkness, Pam turned and saw the vague outline of her friend on the trail.

"I don't know where we are," she panted, exasperation and exhaustion hollowing her voice.

Terra leaned down and rested her hands on her knees, catching her breath. "I think . . . we need . . . to veer off . . . to the left." Her answer came in spurts. They had run hard and fast, but they were on neither a logging road nor a trail.

Just exactly where they were, neither woman could determine with certainty.

Terra's heart continued its percussion in her ears. She swallowed hard. Sticking to the roof of her mouth, her tongue was thick with dehydration. And her shoulders cramped from running with her fully loaded backpack strapped on.

Something clobbered against her pack. The impact sent her lurching to the ground, knocking the wind from her lungs.

"Terra!" Pam ran toward her.

"Keep . . . going . . ." Her voice came in panting gasps as Terra struggled to catch her breath. She was being dragged to her feet, roughly and quickly. Her nostrils were assailed with the odor of her captor.

"Now, you don't want to leave us, do you, girlie?" Leon's rasping, sarcastic voice pierced the blackness. "You better help your friend up. And then you're gonna come back to the cabin. I guess you need to learn a lesson about running away." His hollow cackle echoed across the trail.

Pam extended a hand and brushed off Terra's shoulder and backpack as Terra straightened. She heard the sharp intake of breath as Terra tried to put her weight on her leg.

"I think I twisted my knee." Terra's voice was ragged. She leaned on Pam and limped toward the cabin. Ahead, the bright halogen lantern sat on an abandoned cable spool in front of the structure.

"Now you girls get in there." Leon pushed Pam into the door. It sprung open with the impact, screeching on rusty hinges. "Don't give us no more trouble, because I've got a gun and I'll use it. You could end up down on the riverbank with a bullet through your brain."

The riverbank . . . bullet . . . Something clicked in Terra's mind. Something reminiscent and horrifying.

"Like the wolf you shot last winter?" She was grasping at straws. Venturing a guess. And holding her breath as she awaited his answer.

"Yep. Just like that!" Leon snapped his fingers under Terra's nose. "Just like that! You been nosin' around where you don't belong, just like that wolf. He kept sneakin' around here at night. Ate half the deer we had hanging out in back. Well, he don't sneak around no more." The man's grease-encrusted shirt stretching over his belly jostled as he laughed.

The slime! Terra felt nauseated, as revulsion flooded through her. This cowardly cretin standing before her was responsible for shooting R-21. For an instant, flashing through her mind was the powerful, majestic wolf, fleeing the enclosure in West Yellowstone the day he was released in the wild. His beauty and dignity, she'd never forget.

The day they had transported his lifeless body from the Madison River to the lab, she had felt a part of her heart go with him. Now, she stood face-to-face with the beautiful animal's executioner.

"Fred, bring the gun. We're gonna have to finish what we started last night. These ladies"—his badly neglected teeth widened into a demented grin as his eyes slithered from Pam to Terra—"just don't know how to stay put. I'm gonna have to teach them a lesson about sneakin' around where they're not invited, just like I did with the big bad wolf." Again, he brayed like a donkey.

His bony companion dug in the tool chest for the gun.

"Where'd ya put the gun last night, Leon?"

"I didn't have it." Leon shook his mangy head. "You had it."

Fred stood gape-jawed. "You had it after I did," he accused.

"Go look for it, you knothead." Leon was as devoid of patience as he was of personality.

They hunted on tabletops and in drawers.

Terra felt Pam's nudge, and followed her eyes to a spot underneath the double sink against one wall. At that moment, both women knew what had dropped to the floor in their attempt to escape. The barrel of the pistol poked out from under the sink's peeling wooden cabinet.

Pam rolled her eyes questioningly and shrugged.

There was no way they could reach the gun. But at least, they wouldn't give its location away to the two miscreants holding them captive.

Both men were too intent on their mission to hear what Terra, with her unusually acute hearing, detected in the distance. The low rumbling droned through the dawn. It was coming nearer.

I know what that is, Terra realized. She corrected herself: *I know* who *it is.*

But if the men holding them hostage heard it, too, it could mean danger.

"I don't know why you won't listen to us. We don't mean any harm. We could even cook breakfast for you if you want," she offered, rambling loudly while Pam looked on with a combination of fascination and disgust.

Was Terra out of her mind? Pam wondered. Had the stress of the situation caused her to snap? Never had Terra babbled as she did now. On and on the woman prattled, professing their innocence, ranting about how uncomfortable her night had been, offering their services as cooks, almost flirting with Leon.

Then Pam heard it, too. The sound carried across the clearing. It was gaining on them.

Terra was trying to create a diversion!

Pam began mumbling and shuffling her feet. She coughed. And then made a big production of yawning. Anything to make a noise and cover the sounds outside.

Only when Terra stopped talking long enough to draw a breath, did the men's attention shift from their captives.

"You hear that, Fred? Somebody's out there."

Both women stood statue-still. Pam glanced at Terra questioningly, and was rewarded with an almost imperceptible nod as Terra sought to reassure her friend.

"You move, and you're dead." After rummaging

through tables full of tools unsuccessfully to find the gun, Fred panicked and held up his hand. One finger pointed at the women like a gun barrel.

If he hadn't been so pathetic, he would have been laughable. Here he was, a grown man, using his hand in place of a gun. Pointing at the women to make them surrender, he again assumed his Clint Eastwood persona.

"Watch his finger, Pam, it might be loaded," Terra observed with a smirk.

Leon crossed in front of his cohort and shoved a fist in front of Terra's face.

"You shut up right now, missy, or I'll wallop you a good one." Clearly, Leon's mission in life was to be the most foul-smelling bully in the neighborhood.

The roar of an engine was right outside the door now.

"Leon, we gotta run!" Fred shouted. "Somebody's coming after us!"

It was precisely at that moment the cabin's occupants heard the dull thud of metal scraping the front wall.

"Run, Leon, run!" Both men scrambled to the door and fought to see who would unbolt it and get out the fastest.

It wasn't fast enough.

With a deafening screech of cracking wood, the front wall of the cabin disintegrated as the blade of a huge logging tractor pushed through it. Splintering timbers flew across the cabin. Exhaust from the machine billowed into the air as the engine revved loudly, like a giant clearing his throat. The blade bit deeper into the cabin.

Shelves buckled.

Tables fell.

Window frames crumbled.

Then, as quickly as it had begun, the grader withdrew. The engine sputtered and shut down. For an instant, the silence was deafening.

Four people stood wide-eyed, watching Wheezer Johannson step down from the operator's seat. In three quick steps, he stood in front of them. Long, muscle-thickened arms, strengthened by years of toting a heavy chainsaw up the mountain, folded around both men's necks.

"That's about all the trouble you're going to cause around here, partner," he growled to Fred.

Leon stared at the tall, hard-hatted logger and cowered. The fat man's face suddenly resembled a balloon with some of the air let out: saggy and deflated.

Dawn had begun breaking, and in the pinkish glow streaming through the trees, Terra saw two familiar trucks parked across the clearing.

Max King and Frank Daniel stood beside their trucks, poised and ready to come to Wheezer's aid if necessary.

Terra looked from Wheezer to her coworkers, then back again.

"You gents better mosey over there and get yourselves in those nice brown trucks." Wheezer's jovial tone held an underlying menace. "The sheriff's coming to pay you a visit real soon, and we don't want you running off before she gets here."

Leon plodded reluctantly toward Max's truck. Fred, taking second position, stared at his feet as he stumbled across the grassy clearing to Frank's truck.

The dust settled. Only then could they see the gaping hole at the cabin's front.

"Wheezer, how in the world did you know we were being held in there?" Terra was grateful, but mystified.

"I didn't know. It was these gents." Wheezer hooked a thumb over his shoulders at the two FWP men behind him. "Seems they knew you two were damsels in distress."

"How—?" Pam began.

"I got worried about you ladies." Max King grinned. "Yesterday afternoon you radioed you were tracking One fifty point six. It was transmitting a mortality signal. When you found the collar and picked it up, the motion started the collar transmitting a regular signal. We were concerned when you didn't come back to the office after sundown, and then we discovered the collar had gone back into a mortality signal. I figured if you were carrying it in your backpack like you usually do, the motion of your body would've kept it on a regular signal. It worried us enough that we started looking for the spot where you last called in. We started following your collar signal on the receiver, but we couldn't pin it down in the dark. Wheezer had seen you heading down the mountain last night. He had a suspicion—''

"Just a feeling deep in my gut," Wheezer interjected.

"—that this cabin might hold the answer," Max finished. "We sneaked up here just about the time you were being herded back in the cabin. We were afraid to try anything. We could see in the window and as soon as I spotted their pistol under the sink in the corner, I knew that they were unarmed. We tried the door but it was locked, so Wheezer decided to employ a little friendly persuasion." His nod toward the demolished wall was accompanied by a grin.

"Looks like I persuaded 'em, all right!" Wheezer beamed.

"Not that a government agency would condone such a thing," Max added with mock severity.

"Absolutely not. Nobody would. It's just that, ya know, I never was any good at parking that skidder," Wheezer responded drolly.

"It's a chop shop," Terra explained. "They made a run last night, probably with a shipment of parts."

Max nodded in confirmation. "One of many runs. The sheriff's office has been aware of their activities but couldn't pin down their location. They've been pretty slippery."

Pam nodded in Leon's direction as he pouted in the truck. "Anything with that much grease on it," she said with disgust, "*would* be slippery."

A board fell off from the fractured cabin wall with a clunk.

"Well, I'm glad I could help the sheriff see things a little better." Wheezer's laugh came clear from his toenails.

"You saved our lives, Wheezer." Terra felt her heart catch in her throat. It had been a long, long night.

"Ah, applesauce. Nothin' you wouldn't do for me, young'un," the old logger dismissed it modestly.

"I'm not sure I'd have the nerve to drive a logging skidder through the wall of a wooden building. It was chancy."

Wheezer shook his head. "Nah. These guys had been watching in the windows and told me nobody was in my way."

"Max, thanks for being on top of things." Terra hugged her supervisor gratefully.

"Does this even things out between you and me, Terra, after I made you dance around in the Monty Moose costume at the fair?" Max posed his question with a tease.

Terra pretended to think on it long and hard. "You know, Max, it would take a mighty big favor to cancel out my afternoon as a moose, but I think maybe you've managed to do it! Consider my favor repaid in full!"

The crunch of tires on rocks in the clearing heralded the arrival of Sheriff Jessell. She stepped out of her car and shook hands all around. It was an election year, and L. N. Jessell never missed a chance to campaign. A skinny, efficient fireball of energy, she coupled feisty determination with a sense of fairness. As the county's first elected female sheriff, she could hold her own against any law enforcement officer in Montana.

"L. N., we've got your car choppers in our trucks." Max pointed to his captives.

"One of them is responsible for shooting R-21, Max. He admitted it to Pam and me." Terra glared toward the truck holding the culprits.

"Doesn't surprise me." Max turned his head and spit into a nearby juniper bush. Dealing with lowlifes such as the two reprobates they had just apprehended left a bad taste in his mouth.

"We'll send a crew in here tomorrow to inventory the contents of that cabin." L. N. tipped back her broad-brimmed Stetson. "Looks like we've got enough to hold those two yahoos for a while."

"Talk to Ted Easton at the Fish, Wildlife & Parks Department, too," Terra suggested. "He'll give you information on the wolf they shot." Just thinking about it infuriated Terra all over again. No punishment could be harsh enough for the poachers.

L. N. narrowed the distance between herself and the two suspects. There was no need for backup as she handcuffed the men and loaded them behind the caged partition in her patrol car. The look of steely determination on her face made Max almost feel sorry for the two men. Almost.

It was in the comfort of her condo that evening when it all hit Terra: being abducted, recalling the fate of R-21, standing next to a wall as a huge piece of equipment roared through it.

What *could* have happened unnerved her more than what did in fact transpire.

The jangling phone interrupted her jitters.

"Hi, Sis!" Willy's voice, warm and soothing as a cocker spaniel, bounced over the line.

"Willy! I was just getting ready to call you."

"Great! So we'll talk on my money instead of yours! I haven't talked to you for nearly a month. I guess you've been awfully busy?"

"Buckle your seat belt, sweetie," Terra teased her brother. "Have I got news for you."

For the next hour, Willy was kept spellbound hearing about Terra's recent adventures.

"So where," Willy needed to know, "is this relationship with your biological grandmother going?"

"I promised to go back the third weekend in August for the Crow Fair. She's a fascinating woman, Willy."

"But we're your family, too." There was an underlying hint of anxiety in his tone. It wasn't like Willy.

"And you always will be. Nothing's going to change that, hon."

"How are Mom and Dad handling your . . . uh, seeking your roots?"

"I haven't talked to them since I got back from the reservation. They're still on vacation in California. But I'm sure they'll be supportive, just like they've always been."

Conversation meandered through the twins' latest accomplishments, to Willy's law practice and Jennifer's work with the New Orleans Symphony Association, and finally on to Terra's deliberately avoided subject.

"Have you talked to Whit lately?"

"No."

"Sis, how can you go on like this? You've got to make a decision. Whit has to be in your life, or out of it."

Willy didn't mention that he'd talked to the object of his sister's heartache. While in Washington, D.C., for a law conference, Willy had called him. Over dinner, Whit admitted his feelings hadn't changed.

"But," Whit had told him honestly and with finality, "I'm not stepping back into her life unless she asks me to. It has to be her decision."

Willy remembered the agony in the man's eyes when he mentioned Terra. How could two people, Willy wondered, be so in love with each other and be hurting each other so completely?

Chapter Ten

Twenty-five. Twenty-six. Now, twenty-seven.

Terra kept count. The twenty-seventh pickup truck haul-ing a horse trailer had just passed her on the highway. Leaving directly from the office had been a good idea. It had bought her another hour of daylight and spared her some of the crush of traffic heading for the Crow Fair. She had stopped in Billings for a quick bite of dinner, then was on her way again.

Twilight was descending slowly, beautifully. On the highway, the early evening's dusk brightened the line of headlights along the road leading to the Crow Reservation. In her rearview mirror, the string of lights behind her stretched out like gleaming amber beads twinkling in the purple, fading light. This was the most traffic she'd ever encountered on the road; it was testament to the Crow Fair's drawing power.

A letter from Neva had outlined her plans for the third weekend in August. As part of the traditional celebration, Alexx Light had erected tepees for Neva and for himself at the fairgrounds. With hundreds of fairgoers similarly housed, the wooded area surrounding the fairgrounds be-came a sea of conical canvas structures, their tepee poles reaching into the sky.

Alexx had called last week to confirm Terra's plans.

"You're still planning to come for the Crow Fair, aren't you?" His voice held the expectant enthusiasm of a young

boy. Having Raymond's daughter at the fair would make
the festival especially meaningful.

Terra's voice trilled with enthusiasm. "I surely am, Uncle Alexx. I'm really looking forward to it."

"We'll be at the fairgrounds, right on the edge of Crow
Agency. Follow the cars. You can't miss it. When you get
to the fairgrounds, ask anybody to show you where our
tepees are. They'll know."

"I'm excited to be a part of it, Alexx." The opportunity
to learn more about the Crow people was important to
Terra. She'd thought long and hard about it. It went without
saying that Mason and Nancy Bartlett would always be her
parents. But in learning the Crow ways, she sought to honor
the memory of the people who had given her life.

"This brings us great joy, Terra. You know, the tribe
lives from one Crow Fair to the next. This year it has special meaning to the old woman and to me because you are
coming home."

Home. Two months ago, it was her most feared place,
the reservation. Now, her blood relatives called it her home.

Another home, she corrected herself. It wasn't the
sprawling ranch house with manicured lawns and "Bartlett" stenciled on the mailbox; where Nancy kept her knit-
ting bag next to the armchair and Mason's history books
lined the walls.

Nor was it the condo where Terra had sponge-painted
the walls and added her own decorative touches; where
pictures of ski weekends with her buddies were plastered
with magnets on the refrigerator door.

It was a different kind of home, this vast country of
rippling grain fields and brightly painted storefronts, of picturesque tepees silhouetted against the orange setting sun.
This was the home of horseback riders crossing the Little
Big Horn River, catching the last rays of sunlight on their
ponies' flanks. This was where cottonwood branches
danced with far-off drums on moonlit nights.

Yes, it was different. But it was another home.

Terra shook herself from her reverie and answered, "Yes, Uncle, I'll see you Friday night."

Alexx's words came back to her now as she followed a car with Oklahoma plates to the fairgrounds turnoff ". . . : *because you are coming home.*"

The overwhelming sense of exhilaration she felt as she saw families bound for the fair, blankets and picnic coolers in hand, astounded her. Picnics were nothing new to the Bartletts. Terra's family had gone to picnics and fairs for years.

But her sense of festivity, her sense of community, had never felt stronger than it did tonight.

She angled her truck into a slot in the dusty parking area and reached for the Levi jacket stowed behind the front seat. It was a hot August night, but in Montana, the temperature seldom stayed up all night. Alexx had warned her that by the time the dancing finished in the early hours of morning, the air would be cool.

Blending in with a sea of fairgoers, she passed booths selling Indian tacos. The enticing aroma of onions, fry bread, tomatoes, and ground beef permeated the air. Other merchants offered snuff can lids for the cone-shaped jingles to decorate dance dresses. Still other stalls sold colorful jewelry, beading, and leatherwork. Art displayed on easels and exhibited on tables attested to the resident talent throughout the reservation.

The crowd thickened as Terra found the center of activity. The tinkling of bells and jingles from dance costumes layered with the shouts of friends spotting friends across the clearing. Car doors slammed. Horses whinnied. Boom boxes blared country and western music. The PA system crackled with jokes and dance contest results and announcements. Babies cried and dogs barked.

Tying together the cacophony was the ever-present heartbeat of drums. Their constant, mellow throbbing pulsated through the night, weaving a spell. Beautiful. Exciting. Welcoming.

Never had Terra seen such diversity. Cowboy hats mingled with feathered headdresses. Young women in buckskin dresses crossed paths with those in denim shorts and halter tops. Old women in polyester pantsuits visited with their counterparts in elk-tooth–trimmed dresses. Rednecks in baseball caps turned backward struck up conversations with weathered-skinned Indian farmers. Gum-popping photographers with equipment clanking from neckstraps fraternized with dignified tribal elders.

Children stood patiently while parents groomed them in readiness for dance contests. One small girl, Terra noted, had three different women pulling at sections of her long, lustrous hair, braiding it into intricate designs. The child looked up and caught Terra watching her. She rolled her eyes indulgently and laughed. Terra shared her mirth.

In another corner, a band of fancy dancers limbered like the athletes they were, bending and stretching to keep their energy up until they were called upon to enter the competition.

"Excuse me." Terra approached one of the men designated as a fair worker. "I was told you could direct me to Alexx Light's tepee."

"Lemmee see . . . Alexx . . . he sets his tepee up in that grove of aspens," the man answered, pointing to the far side of the grounds.

"Thanks." Terra smiled.

Throughout the fairgrounds, lawn chairs were pulled into circles. Visitors of every age renewed acquaintances and caught up on news. The Crow Fair was equal parts family reunion, country social, craft market, dance competition, and rodeo.

In the circles of light thrown by camp lanterns, old men with skin like crimped leather squatted close to the ground in huddles, gambling with sticks. Their raucous laughter and rapid-fire Crow language added to the kaleidoscopic sound of the festival.

Rows of tepees, rising from the grassy field like immense

pointed mushrooms, were edged with similarly dense rows of camp trailers, pickups with camper shells, and tents.

Glowing from lanterns within, the tepees spilled their golden light into the darkness. As each tepee's occupants moved around inside, ghostlike shadows danced across the stretched canvas. The entire area was bathed in a surrealistic radiance.

Terra scanned the crowd in the vicinity of Alexx's tepee. For the first time in her life, she was looking at a sea of faces like her own. The color of her skin wasn't the exception in this group; it was the norm. She had seldom felt out of place in the white world; still, she gloried in the lack of curiosity in the eyes of people she now passed. She was a Crow; they were Crows. She may be new to them, but she was not different.

As her glance skimmed the groups sitting outside the tepees, it caught and held on the stately woman seated at the end of the path in front of her.

"Kaalá!" Terra's voice was lost in the commotion. Her stride lengthened, quickly covering the distance between them. She dropped to one knee and put her arms around the old woman in the lawn chair. "I'm glad to see you, Kaalá."

"It is good to see you, Terra," the old woman responded. Her hand smoothed Terra's silky braid lovingly. Dancing eyes in the age-sculptured face confirmed the old woman's joy. "No trouble on the highway? Is your truck running all right?"

"Just fine. There are so many cars on the interstate, I felt like part of a caravan coming here. How are you, Kaalá? Are you well?"

"I am very well. Having you here makes my heart sing."

Her grandmother, filled with pride, introduced Terra to the group of old women sitting in a circle.

"This is Terisa and Raymond's daughter," she explained.

"She is a beauty, like her mother," a wrinkled, smiling sprite remarked.

Another old woman took Terra's hand. "It is good that you have come home to your people."

A group of horsemen, young Crow men riding bareback, disrupted the camp as they wound through the tepees and kicked up dust. Their exuberant shouting and laughter, along with a gritty film of dust, settled on everything as they reined in their horses, turned, and galloped toward the riverbank.

"It is fair time," Neva announced with a smile, as if to excuse their rowdiness. "Happiness is everywhere at fair time."

"Is this your tepee?" Terra rose, admiring the structure looming behind her grandmother.

"It is. Alexx has always spent fair time in a tepee. This year, he asked me to stay, too. He thought you would enjoy learning some of the traditional ways. Come in." The old woman rose and gathered her shawl from the back of the chair. Nodding toward the tepee, she explained, "I closed it to keep out dust, not people." She didn't want to appear inhospitable; the door to a Crow home was always open to guests.

Terra ducked her head slightly to follow Neva through the opening in the canvas. Inside, the lantern's rose glow intensified the cozy atmosphere of the shelter.

Impressing Terra was both the roominess and the efficiency of the space. Two sleeping bags, rolled and tied, lay on spotless thick rugs spread on the ground. A folding aluminum picnic table stood against one canvas wall. Covering the table were a two-burner propane camp stove and a metal washbasin. A plastic squeeze bottle of dishwashing detergent peeked from behind the filled basin. Under the table, a variety of picnic coolers and water jugs nestled together. Spanning the kitchen area, a makeshift clothesline was draped with damp towels. Two folding lawn chairs bordered a small wooden table.

Opposite the eating area, an old-fashioned leather suitcase sat upright. On top of it rested a tube of toothpaste and a bar of hand soap in a vinyl travel kit.

As a youngster, Terra had spent long, happy hours in a treehouse Mason had built in their backyard. Now, the same sense of adventurous domesticity washed over her.

Yes, it was another home.

"Sit down, child. I'll offer you some herbal tea. Or lemonade? I have lemonade as well."

"Lemonade would be wonderful. Is Alexx around, Kaalá?"

"He's over in the arena with the men. Tomorrow afternoon is the rodeo, and Alexx has entered the relay race. The men are planning their strategy." She laughed. "He said he'd be back about ten o'clock because he hoped you'd arrive by then."

Terra glanced at her wristwatch. She'd made good time. It was just nine-thirty now.

"Or if you like, we can walk over by the rodeo arena and see him."

"I would enjoy that. It would give me a chance to see more of the festivities. But Kaalá, aren't you tired? It's getting late . . ." *For someone your age,* Terra didn't add.

"When fair time comes," Neva said with a laugh, "all other time goes up in smoke. There is no such thing as tired. There is only the fair! Let's go join the festivities."

Alexx Light leaned with his back against the loading chute, his cowboy boot heel hooked onto a rung of the fence. He listened to first one, and then another of his childhood chums brag about their horsemanship skills. A part of the tradition of the rodeo riders, it was what Alexx imagined psychologists would call a male bonding experience.

It was good to be with his friends at the time-honored tradition of the Crow Fair. They had been boys together on the reservation, then had grown and gone their separate ways to college, the military, careers. But each year, the

draw of the fair pulled them back to the reservation. He
was one of the lucky ones who'd been able to stay behind
and earn a good living in the place that held his heart.

A group of cowboys from the other side of the reservation had gathered near the livestock pens. Tossing greetings
back and forth with Alexx's group, they continued mulling
around the pens.

Whit Bull Chief glanced up and pushed the cowboy hat
back on his head. Something about the tall, angular man
by the chutes looked familiar.

"Hey, Neville. Who's the guy in the black shirt?" Whit
nodded across the pen.

Neville Tall Bear squinted into the circle of light thrown
from an overhead fixture.

"That's Alexx Light. He's a building contractor from
Staghorn. His brother Raymond and my father went to
school together."

Concentration furrowed Whit's brow. Something gnawed
at his stomach when he looked at Alexx Light. Something
about the man stirred him up and riled him to the core. But
what was it?

"You want me to make an introduction for you?" Neville was the self-appointed hospitality chairman of the fair.
Having never left the reservation in his life, he knew everyone. And he wanted everyone else to know everyone, too.

"No." Whit shook his head.

"He's a good man, you know. I kid him a little," Neville
went on. "I tell him he drives that fancy sports car of his
just as fast as he drives his horses."

The sports car.

The man under the porch light.

The man with Terra.

"He got a girlfriend?" Whit couldn't stop himself from
asking.

"By golly, he does now. After all these years of being
single, he's found the woman for him. She doesn't live on
the reservation, though."

"Oh?" *Don't let it get to you,* Whit warned himself.

"No." Neville's sources were impeccable. "But I hear he might even be getting married next year."

Whit's jaw clenched like a pit bull with a bone. The muscles in his chiseled face were defined, pulsating. No other visible sign of emotion escaped him.

Neville moved from the stock pens, continuing to prattle to anybody who would listen, as he skipped from tomorrow's weather forecast to predicting the dance contest winners. Sometimes Neville talked even when he knew nobody was listening. He just liked to talk.

Alexx Light turned from his contemporaries, from the "rodeo old-timers" as he knew some of the young bucks called his group, and looked up in time to catch the stranger's glacial stare.

There was no mistaking the look of pure venom in the younger man's glare.

Alexx sought to placate the angry stranger. Maybe the young fellow had been slapped with an ornery stick. Alexx hoped he could square things. The fair was no place for hard feelings; it was for fellowship and celebration.

He ambled toward the corner of the stock area where his would-be adversary was wiping his leather tack with exaggerated concentration.

"I haven't met you before. I'm Alexx Light." He offered his hand, rawly conscious of the other man's intense dislike.

The younger man hesitated. Reluctance claimed him. A split second later, good breeding overruled his sore temper as he shook Alexx's hand firmly.

"Whit Bull Chief." He squared his chin, suggesting a challenge.

Each scoped out the opponent, eyes locked. The undercurrent of apprehension coming from the younger man was palpable.

"You entering the events tomorrow?"

Whit nodded. "The three-horse relay. You?"

"Yeah. The same. My friends have all been at it for years, but this is my first time in the rodeo. I'm a little too old for this." Alexx laughed, a touch of cynicism tainting his humor. He ducked his head and self-consciously pawed a line of dirt with the side of his boot.

Whit's glance was searing. "When a man takes that kind of chance, it usually means there's a female he's trying to impress." He held his breath, waiting for Alexx Light's answer.

"Yeah, you could say that. Her name is Terra." Alexx's grin transformed his face. "She's pretty special in my life."

Yours, too? Whit bit back the words.

She should be here soon, Alexx realized. He stepped back and turned to leave. "Well, good luck tomorrow," he added over his shoulder.

"You, too," Whit heard himself answer, wondering where his voice came from when he felt completely hollow inside.

The older man had the confident saunter of a person in control of his life, Whit realized as he watched Alexx Light cross the dusty farmyard and return to the fairgrounds.

And why shouldn't he?

He had the one thing Whitman Bull Chief needed to make his life complete. He had Terra. And if Alexx Light was riding tomorrow to impress her, Whit realized, it meant only one thing.

It meant that Terra would be here on the reservation, at the Crow Fair, tomorrow.

Give her up, fool, Whit chided himself as he walked back to his family's tepee. *She wouldn't come to the reservation for you.* But she was coming for Alexx Light.

Give her up.

Alexx strode into the throng of fairgoers. He pulled back his shirtsleeve and checked the lighted dial of his watch again. Terra should be here at any minute. Funny, Alexx thought as he smiled and acknowledged old friends in the crowd, how he'd looked forward to showing her the fair traditions. Overwhelmed by his love for his little niece, and the sense of family she'd brought back into his life, he searched the crowd.

"There he is, Kaalá!" Terra spotted the tall cowboy silhouetted against the lights from the dance contest arena.

"Uncle Alexx!" Her long legs carried her quickly to him, and she engulfed him in a bear hug.

Alexx twirled her around and set her back on her feet. "Welcome to the Crow Fair, Terra!" He smiled down at her, at the face so like his beloved brother's.

"This is all so exciting," she chirped as she laced an arm through his and put the other around her grandmother's shoulder. "I can't wait to see the dancers."

"The women's jingle dress dancing is about to begin. Shall we go watch?" Alexx's suggestion was twofold: it was the most beautifully energetic of the dances, and it was also the dance Terisa Old Elk had performed at her last Crow Fair.

Like so many vibrantly colored birds, the dancers circled the arena. The downbeat of the drums complemented the jingling from the dresses much as the bass and treble notes of a song carry each other. Light and airy, the sound of the jingles sprinkled the air like windchimes on a soft breeze. Originating as an Ojibwa dance used in healing, the jingle dress dance had evolved into a colorful competition event.

Next, with a flurry of swaying yarn fringe, the men grass dancers took over. Twisting and turning, they resembled a sea of prairie grass, undulating in the wind.

The last time she had witnessed the frenetic grass dancers, Terra remembered, Whit had been at the Powwow with her. He never left her thoughts for long, and right now his image was pushing across her mind with the subtlety of a jumbo jet.

"...or have you been hypnotized by the grass dancers?"

Alexx was talking to her, and her mind was on something else. Somebody else.

"I'm sorry, Uncle. I didn't hear you." She leaned closer to him and concentrated on his words.

"I just said, you were staring so intently, are you getting tired or just hypnotized by the dancers?"

"It's the dancers." She grinned. "But what about Grandmother? Is she getting tired?" Terra looked around her uncle to where Neva sat on the bleachers, watching the dancers with a look of sheer rapture.

"Neva will never tire of the fair. Long after you and I give in, she will still be enjoying the festivities!" Alexx nodded toward the old woman, whose eyes never left the dancers.

Midnight came and went. The drums continued as one group of singers and then another offered songs. Surrounding elk-hide–covered drums, the singers beat their rhythms in unison and sang out in full volume.

At last, the dancers fell still. Children grew quiet. One by one, they dropped at their parents' feet on folded blankets, and fell asleep. The drums mimicking Mother Earth's heartbeat ceased their throb. Families walked quietly through the night to their tepees while overhead, the quarter moon kept its silvery vigil.

The morning sun crept over slanting canvas tepee walls and brushed Terra's eyelashes with golden warmth. She flipped on her back in the sleeping bag and pulled the back of her hand over her eyes.

A split second's disorientation vanished as she raised her head and spotted Neva kneeling on the floor. The old woman's strong hands were quietly rolling her sleeping bag into a tight bundle.

At the same time, the old woman cocked her head, her attention outside the tepee.

"Listen," she whispered, "the camp crier is coming."

Gearing down, a pickup truck rolled through the encampment, its driver shouting wakeup calls in Crow through speakers mounted on the cab.

Responses pelted the air as good-natured ribbing greeted the crier. It was part of the fair tradition. In a flash, the pickup disappeared into the trees, leaving a wake of laughter and wide-awake campers.

Breakfast was prefaced by industrial-strength coffee. When Alexx joined them, Terra and Neva dispensed shredded hash browns and fry bread with thickly sliced bacon.

"Are you ready to continue your fair orientation?" Alexx couldn't wait to introduce Terra to his friends. Raymond's daughter had come home.

"Very ready." Terra's enthusiasm was contagious. "Explain everything to me, Alexx. You, too, Kaalá!"

"Much of our history is oral, handed down from generation to generation by word," Neva explained as they came across symbols pertinent to the tribe. "Very little of our culture has been written. It is the obligation of parents to teach their children through stories and songs."

Terra's hunger for knowledge as the day wore on was fed as Alexx and Neva took turns explaining, answering questions, and laughing with their inquisitive young woman.

At one of the sale booths, Terra bought an intricately beaded necklace for Nancy. At another, they admired leather goods decorated with minutely braided horse hair.

It was at a jewelry vendor's display that Terra found a pair of earrings for Neva.

"Please, Kaalá," Terra cajoled, "let me buy these for you?"

"I would be honored," Neva responded quietly. Her dignity never failed to impress her granddaughter.

"And a pair for my niece," Alexx instructed the woman in the booth. "Whatever she chooses."

"I would be honored," Terra parroted her grandmother,

hoping to someday attain the same degree of dignity the old woman projected. She pointed to a pair of silver circles glistening in the sun. "Those are beautiful."

"They're yours." Alexx closed the deal and smiled at his brother's child.

"Thank you, Uncle."

"Stand still and hold your hair up," Alexx bossed affectionately. Terra's hair hung loose in a silky curtain down her back today. Her beauty had not escaped the young men at the fair, her uncle realized. He couldn't have been more proud, had Terra been his own daughter. "Let's see those ears of yours and I'll put them on for you."

Terra turned her face up toward Alexx, and grinned as she pulled her hair up and away from her earlobes. He found the spot in each earlobe where the piercing wire caught, and locked the jewelry in place.

"You're wonderful." Terra's arms circled his waist for a heartfelt hug. The happiness of being part of this family couldn't elude her. If she had known them every year since she was born, she could not have felt more comfortable, more secure than she did with Alexx and Neva right now.

She pulled away, and turned back to where Neva stood behind her. But her glance continued past her grandmother and came screeching to a halt on the rough-hewn jawline so familiar to the woman who loved it.

Watching her from the shade of a cottonwood arbor, obsidian eyes bore through Terra with an intensity that took her breath away. Her skin tingled with the sensation of his gaze.

"Whit!" Terra's voice quivered, barely more than a whisper. Her eyes widened with surprise.

Alexx and Neva saw, rather than heard, her plea. Their eyes followed hers to the Crow man standing in the shade.

"I'm, uh, it's . . . I have to see someone." Not since he had met her had Alexx seen Terra so flustered. She stood rubbing one thumbnail against the other, looking from her grandmother to her uncle and back again.

Whit. Whit Bull Chief, Alexx remembered. He'd met the young man last night, and hadn't been all that impressed. Never had he seen so much unfounded anger in anyone. And now it turned out he was a friend of Terra's?

No, Alexx realized, Whit Bull Chief was not a casual friend. The strain in his niece's voice, the tension around her mouth and eyes, told it all. Her hands were clenched into fists, her knuckles bony white. This man was far more to his niece than a casual friend.

For an instant, Terra wavered indecisively. She stood motionless. Then, squaring her shoulders, she walked gracefully to where the young Indian man stood stoically observing her every move.

Chapter Eleven

The haunting beauty of her eyes appealed to Whit with the vulnerability they indicated. He had seen that beauty often enough. Too often, in fact. Every night, it occupied his dreams.

He had watched her interact with the man he met last night. The sun glistened in her hair, cascading down to her waist in its thick, black glory.

But it was more than the eyecatching beauty of her face or figure that made it impossible for Whit to look away from her, walk away from her. It was her vitality, the fire within her that branded a mark on him and fascinated him.

Her face was flushed; whether from the oppressing afternoon sun or from the excitement of the fair, he couldn't determine.

What worried Whit the most, was that maybe her radiance stemmed from something—or somebody—else.

When Alexx Light fit the earrings on Terra, it had wrenched Whit's heart. The gesture was so loving, so intimate. Then she had thrown her arms around the older man and her embrace had been happily reciprocated. It was almost more than Whit could watch, yet he forced himself to do so. He couldn't take his eyes off her, off the woman he loved.

Now she stood before him.

"How are you, Whit?"

"How am I, Terra?" His voice was low, seething with raw control. An undercurrent of cynicism rippled through

152

it. His words were barely audible above the din of the fair crowd; still, Terra heard every syllable. "I'm surprised. That's how I am. I'm amazed that somebody who hated the Crow Reservation as much as you did just months ago, could suddenly show up here laughing and acting like this is your second home. I asked you to come and meet my people, but you wouldn't do it. I practically begged you. Yet now you're here with—" He jerked his head toward the spot where Alexx stood. "—with him. That pretty well tells it all, doesn't it?" With his thumbs hooked in the corner of his Levi's pockets, he stood with legs planted apart, ready for a confrontation.

"I can explain everything, Whit. Please, come and meet Alexx," Terra implored him. "He's—"

Whit's hand flew up, with his palm pointed toward Terra to stop her. "I met him last night," he interrupted. "He's your choice, not mine. Have a nice life, Terra."

He turned on his heel and disappeared into the crowd, leaving the woman who loved him overflowing with confusion.

Over and over in her head, she had replayed what she'd say to Whit when she next saw him. She had affirmed to herself, when she and Pam were held captive in that cabin, that her life would be different if they survived.

It would, she had promised herself, be fuller. She would make peace with her birth family. She would do more for her community. And she would let Whit know that she loved him with all her heart.

Now, she watched his broad shoulders retreating as he made his way through the crowd, distancing himself from her physically, as he was trying to do emotionally.

What had gone so wrong? She wanted him to meet her uncle. The look of pure dislike he had flashed at Alexx was uncalled for. What had precipitated it? Terra shrugged helplessly and walked back to where Neva and Alexx stood waiting.

"I'm sorry." Her apology was unnecessary, she knew.

Her uncle and grandmother could clearly sense her discomfort. "I guess Whit was in a hurry."

"Whit? Is that the Bull Chief boy you mentioned?" Neva picked up on the name immediately.

"Yes. It's been a while since I've seen him. I guess he wasn't very happy to see me."

They continued to make their way toward the rodeo arena, where Alexx would be competing at three-thirty.

Neva's lips pursed to tsk-tsk. "I think," she ventured in her inimitably calm manner, "he isn't very happy with himself."

"I thought it would bring him happiness, seeing me on the reservation, Kaalá. That's all he wanted when we were together. But the way he looked, you'd think it's the very last place he wants me to be. I can't figure him out."

"Do you want me to have a talk with him?" Alexx volunteered. The girl had no father to speak on her behalf. Alexx readily accepted his familial responsibilities.

Terra shook her head furiously. "No. Absolutely not. Whatever has him so angry, he'll have to work through."

"Love can work through anything." Neva smiled enigmatically. That young man loved her granddaughter, and Terra loved him. It was as easy to see as a black bear at a currant bush. Things would work out.

The old woman nodded to herself as she unfolded her blanket over the wooden bleacher and settled in to watch the rodeo.

The smell of sawdust and livestock mingled with rodeo dust as Alexx Light led his gleaming quarter horse toward the group of relay riders. Trip Yellowtail and Luther Crawford held his other two horses in readiness.

Trip had won the steer-wrestling event earlier in the day, and was still reveling in his victory. Luther's stint on the bucking bronco he drew had been less successful; the horse was a twister and had sent the cowboy flying in what could be paraphrased as "toes over teakettle" into the dust.

"Got your number?" Trip checked his friend's back. The entry number safety-pinned on Alexx's shirt would allow judges to identify him during the competition. "Ready?"

Alexx nodded. "I think I'm as ready as I'm ever going to be. Why in the heck I let you guys talk me into this, I'll never know." A craggy grin tugged at one leathery cheek.

"Because next year at this time, you'll be an old married man and your wife won't let you do anything so foolhardy." Trip's laugh came out a cackle. "And besides, 'Uncle Alexx' wants to show off for his niece."

"I guess that's it." Alexx flashed a broad, reckless smile. He knew his buddy had hit the nail on the head. If Terra was going to experience the excitement of the rodeo, how better than for him to be a participant?

The PA system sputtered to life, requesting all relay racers to take their places.

"This is it." Alexx mounted his horse bareback in a single bound, and flashed a thumbs-up signal as his two compadres followed close behind with the backup horses in tow.

The rodeo bleachers were filled to capacity. Sun glared off the windshields of vehicles parked across the fence at the far end of the arena. Horses sidestepped impatiently. It was getting hot, and Alexx felt sweat trickle down the back of his neck.

Six riders lined up abreast of the starting point. Awaiting the signal to begin, Alexx's glance swept to his left and then his right.

Three of the other riders he recognized. The fourth was a stranger, and in the fifth slot was Whit Bull Chief, looking even more menacing than he had last night.

Alexx shifted his weight. His muscles were tight. Beneath his thighs, the horse's rock-hard back was sweaty and made him itch.

Anticipation knotted Alexx's stomach muscles and set his hands trembling.

The signal blasted.

His horse bolted, pulling ahead of those on either side of him. Flying on long, powerful strides, the horse was in complete control.

On the far left, Alexx was vaguely aware of another rider pulling ahead. Dust enveloped the group as they headed into the first turn.

The world became a blur of thundering hooves and the taste of dust as they rounded the curve and picked up speed on the straightaway. Nearing the starting point, the lead rider began his dismount. As quickly as he pulled a leg over his horse, his handlers were there with the next mount. The man scrambled onto the back of the second horse and continued his frenetic pace.

Close behind him, Alexx saw Trip ready to hand over the horse for the next leg of the relay. Alexx was down in an instant, grappling with the reins of his second horse.

Up onto the horse's back he went. The transition from the quarter horse to the buckskin was accomplished quickly, smoothly.

Again the riders neared the curve. In a haze of dust, Alexx could make out a rider pulling in front of them. Hooves pounded into the track, the steady beat matching the percussion of his heart. In a flash, he recognized Whit Bull Chief as the rider moving into second place.

Out of the turn, the horses galloped at full speed, manes flying and nostrils flaring with the exhilaration of the run.

The second handoff was under way, with Whit Bull Chief still in second position and Alexx close behind.

Alexx's leg muscles were cramping. Bareback riding was an art. With no saddle to distribute the rider's weight, all balance was left to the knees and thighs. Alexx was more accustomed to unleashing the horsepower in his car than clamping himself barebacked onto a horse. That lack of training was telling on him as he struggled to maintain his posture on the horse.

* * *

In the stands, Terra had recognized both men as they entered the arena.

How ironic, she thought, watching her first Crow Fair Rodeo, and having two men she cared deeply about, competing against each other!

Her pride in Alexx mingled with a stronger sentiment. This man's blood was her blood; looking at him gave her an idea of what her own father must've looked like. In the pictures of Raymond that Alexx had given her, he looked very young.

He *was* young when he died in the house fire, Terra realized. He was twenty-seven: the same age as she was right now.

And all that remained of him, of his blood, was Alexx and herself. The bond between them was a treasured one.

She watched now as the riders completed their second handoff and sped down the track.

Whit was clearly the better horseman. He was one with his horse, gracefully controlling the animal with seemingly small effort. He glided across the arena like a feather on the wind. It was easy, Terra realized, to envision him as a warrior one hundred years ago, galloping across the prairie in battle. Seeing him like this stirred deep emotions within her. *This is the man I love,* she wanted to shout to the world.

Alexx, on the other hand, was working hard. As the riders crossed in front of the bleachers, Terra could see sheer determination contorting his usually cheerful face into a hard mask of concentration. His riding was labored, at one point almost clumsy.

Be careful, Uncle, she pleaded under her breath. *You don't have to prove anything to me to be my hero. You already are.*

Neva leaned forward, totally engrossed in the action on the track. She had witnessed countless relays at the rodeo; they never failed to intrigue her.

The racers rounded the second turn and headed toward

the handoff point. The final set of horses had been led out and stood ready for their riders.

Up ahead, Alexx saw Luther and Trip struggling to control his third mount. The horse was skittery, tossing its head in an attempt to brake halter. At the same time, the cowboy could feel his leg cramping with a vicious stab.

"Hold him!" Alexx's breath was ragged as he yelled to Luther. He could see that Whit Bull Chief had just completed his third handoff and was on his way into the last lap.

Alexx reined in his horse and began the transfer to his final mount. Sliding off the big animal's back, he hit the ground too hard and grappled to maintain his balance. A lurch forward propelled him against the waiting horse. Skittery, the horse shifted its hind legs.

As his leg went over the back of the final mount, Alexx boosted himself forward to swing his full weight onto the animal. The smell of horse sweat assailed his nostrils as he clung to the animal. His leg felt like it was being skewered with a hot poker.

What happened next would be hashed over again and again, being retold to the point of exhaustion by the cowboys witnessing the accident.

Whether the third horse attempted to rear up, or whether he merely sidestepped and dumped his rider, no one was certain. It happened so quickly, in a heartbeat of blurred action.

All that was clear was the rider went down, thrown onto the track. The last two riders, now coming into the handoff area, were traveling too fast to swerve.

In a flurry of kicking hooves and flailing arms, the fourth rider and his horse went down. Dust shrouded the scene, momentarily obliterating everything and adding to the mayhem.

Terra flew out of her seat the instant she saw Alexx struggling to control his horse. By the time he hit the ground, she was already out of the bleachers and running toward him.

The lead riders were in the far corner of the track, seemingly unaware of the chaos behind them. They rounded the corner. Above the din of beating hooves, Whit heard a roar.

From the crowd's reaction, Whit knew something had happened behind him. He turned, looking over his shoulder at the handoff point, where two horses and their riders were down. In the same instant, his peripheral vision caught Terra running across the track.

"Terra! Stay away!" His shouts were lost in the hoofbeats of his horse and the noise of the crowd.

No! No! No! Terra's mind screamed at Alexx as she crossed the track in panic. *Don't be hurt! Don't die! You can't die!*

He lay on the dusty field, the blood from his mouth oozing red down his cheek and into the dirt under his head. His lips were colorless, his eyes closed.

"No," Terra crooned, sobbing, as she reached him. "No, Alexx."

Dropping to her knees beside him, she gently placed her hand under his. Whispering softly to him, her tears dripped onto the arm of his shirt as she repeated over and over, "It'll be all right. You'll be okay, you'll be okay."

The wail of an ambulance grew ever closer, as cowboys mingled helplessly around the supine rider.

A horse reined in close behind Terra, and the rider dismounted in one smooth motion. His shadow fell across Alexx as he hovered above the injured man. After making a quick assessment of the unconscious figure before him, the cowboy dusted his hands together, wiped them on his thighs, and straightened.

Strong arms pulled Terra to her feet.

"He's going to be all right." Whit gathered her tightly against him, cradling her head to his shoulder. "He's got the wind knocked out of him and he probably chewed a chunk out of his tongue, but he'll be all right. They'll get him to the hospital and check him over, but he's not going to die.''

He leaned back from the waist and looked into her eyes. One hand came up to brush a trail of tears from her cheek.

Her emotions were running as fast as the relay horses. Here she was crying over her uncle, whispering prayers for his recovery. And now, Whit's arms were encircling her.

''Will he really be all right?'' Her voice cracked as the tears started again. ''He can't die, Whit. He's just got to be all right. I love him and I need him.'' She buried her head against Whit's hard-muscled shoulder.

What she missed was the tortured look that washed over Whit's face, darkening his expression. It was a mistake to hold her again, Whit knew. But he had known from the moment he saw her at the fairgrounds that having her in his arms again was all he wanted.

The ambulance crew loaded Alexx carefully. The emergency van pulled away from the rodeo grounds, its siren screeching under the cloudless blue sky as it sped toward the hospital.

''Come on.'' Whit stepped back, keeping an arm around Terra's waist. ''I'll take you to the hospital so you can be with him.''

''Wait a minute, please? I need to get my bag.'' She ran across the track to where Neva sat, patiently awaiting word on her friend's condition.

''Kaalá, I'm going to the hospital to check on Alexx. Do you want to ride with us?''

''You go ahead.'' Neva grasped her hand and squeezed it reassuringly. ''He is your blood. Hurry and be with him. I'll catch a ride later.''

A quick hug for Neva, and Terra was off, bounding across the field on those long legs. On the other side of the track, Neva smiled. For some reason, she knew Alexx was going to be all right. Everything was going to be all right.

* * *

The antiseptic smell pervading the hospital corridor prickled at their noses as Whit and Terra found the emergency room waiting area and checked in with the receptionist on duty. They sat quietly as the attending nurse squished down the hall on thick crepe-soled shoes. In just a moment, she returned, smiling.

"Mr. Light will need to have a few stitches in his lip. It seems in the accident his mouth connected with a horse hoof and the horse won. And there's a little matter of a broken arm that needs to be set. But he'll be assigned a room for the night and you're welcome to visit him there. It'll be about an hour."

Retreating to her station, the nurse quickly immersed herself in paperwork. The ticking clock was the only sound in the waiting room.

"Would you like a cup of coffee?" Whit's voice broke the silence.

"Thanks. No." Terra rubbed her thumbnails across each other nervously.

"It's going to be okay, Terra." He picked up her hand and laced his fingers through hers. He hadn't forgotten the pleasure he derived from her touch. His feelings for her had only grown stronger while they'd been apart.

"I know." She nodded and brushed her cheek against one shoulder. "I'm sorry. I'm acting like a baby."

"No, I don't think you are."

"I am. I know it. But I can't imagine my life without him now."

The pain Alexx Light was suffering right now, Whit realized, couldn't be hurting any more than what he himself was living through, hearing Terra profess her love for the older man.

Still, loving her as he did, Whit couldn't let her go through this alone.

"Tell me about Alexx."

"He's fun and caring and hard working," Terra sniffed between sobs. "And he's been so good to me."

"He'd better be," Whit responded, more to himself than to her.

The automatic double doors leading to the emergency room swished open.

A middle-aged couple peered into the room, the man removing his baseball cap and exposing long black braids, as he looked around for a familiar face. Finding none, he stepped back to admit a third party.

Neva Old Elk, head erect and shoulders proudly back, entered.

"Kaalá! We're over here." Terra rose from the waiting room couch and crossed the room to escort the old woman to a seat.

Kaalá?

Whit's limited knowledge of Crow included familiar words, words a family used in everyday life. He recognized the term his sisters used to address their grandmother.

Kaalá.

The old woman took her place in a vinyl chair by the window and stared straight ahead.

Terra's hand caressed the woman's shoulder as she stood over her, looking from the old woman to Whit.

"Kaalá, this is Whitman Bull Chief. Whit, this is my grandmother, Neva Old Elk."

A hint of a smile pulled at Terra's lips. Her eyes were luminous as they went from the old woman's face to Whit's.

Whit stood up and took the gnarled, strong hand in his. "I'm pleased to meet you, Mrs. Old Elk."

"I've heard many good things about you from my grand-daughter," Neva returned.

"When did you . . .?" Whit was mystified. His eyes traced a path between Terra and the old woman. Terra's grandmother? So she had searched out her birth parents.

"Last month," Terra answered. "I petitioned the court and they appointed an intermediary who contacted Grandmother."

"And your parents? Have you met them, too? Where are they?" Pride in Terra's courage was infused with the love Whit felt for her.

"They died soon after I was born," Terra answered softly, glancing at Neva.

The old woman's look of peace never wavered.

"I had a vision my granddaughter would come back home, and now she is here." Neva's voice held a note of conviction. She trusted her visions.

Whit sat very still, trying to digest the information he'd been given. After years of wondering about her birth parents, Terra had learned the truth.

What peace it must have brought her.

An intercom buzzed in the nurses' station. A moment later, the nurse poked her head into the waiting room.

"Miss Bartlett? Mr. Light has been transferred to a regular room now. You're welcome to go see him for a few minutes if you like."

Terra turned to Neva. "Do you want to come with me, Kaalá?"

Brushing the young woman off with one hand, Neva declined. "He will want to see you first. Go to him. I'll follow with Mr. and Mrs. KnowsGuns." Neva indicated the couple who had accompanied her to the hospital.

Two pairs of coal black eyes watched the beautiful young woman leave the room.

"Alexx Light was foolish to ride in the relay." Neva's voice, although soft, resonated in the stark silence of the waiting room. She shook her head slowly, bewildered.

"This is my tenth year in relays. I've gotten to know most of the riders." Whit stood up and stretched taller. Flexing his tight shoulder muscles, he ran his palms down the thighs of his dusty jeans. He squinted out the window, over the vast open field skirting the hospital grounds. His sigh was ragged and weary. "I've never seen him participate in one before."

"He's never been much for riding in the rodeo. Machinery always fascinated him." Neva's chuckle was hearty. "He'd much rather drive his fancy sports car than ride one of his ponies."

"But he rode in the relay. Was it because of Terra?"

"Yes. He wanted to make her first Crow Fair memorable."

When Whit made no comment, Neva added, "He's certainly done that."

They fell into silence, with Whit's frown reflected in the window glass and Neva lost in thought.

Five minutes went by. Then five more.

"Alexx is bandaged up and doing just fine, Kaalá." Terra bounced into the waiting room, her smile telling it all. "Why don't you go say hello to him?"

"Perhaps I will do that. Then Mr. and Mrs. KnowsGuns will take me back to the encampment," Neva answered.

Terra nodded her agreement. "I'll go back with Whit now if you don't mind, and get my truck. That way I can come back later tonight and see Alexx again."

Whit prayed for the wisdom of the great chiefs. If there was any way he could keep Terra from coming back to the hospital tonight, maybe, just maybe, he could win her love away from Alexx Light.

Chapter Twelve

It was nearly eight o'clock when Whit pulled off the high-way and found a parking spot at the fairgrounds. The early-evening sun bronzed the trees along the Little Big Horn River and turned the water to molten gold. A gentle breeze fanned Terra's hair as she stepped out of the car and slammed the door.

"What a beautiful evening!" She flashed a radiant smile at Whit, a smile that tied itself around his heart and tugged for all it was worth.

Any evening with her was beautiful, Whit determined. When she laughed, it was like the gentle rains of spring-time, fresh and nourishing and filled with the hope of life.

"Looks like the rodeo's still going on," Whit observed. A cloud of dust above the arena signaled yet another event on the bone-dry track. "How about a walk down by the river? It'll be a little cooler." *Say yes,* he pleaded silently.

"Yes."

Yes! Whit's heart soared. *Yes!*

They stepped through tall grass on the embankment and walked to where the high-water mark met the finely gran-ulated river sand on the beach.

The river was down now, after being swollen in early summer from snow runoff in the mountains. The Little Big Horn was a picturesque river; undeveloped, it retained its rustic charm. Age-old cottonwoods bent over the riverbank, their greenery-laden limbs shading portions of the water and rendering a cool respite from the hot, dusty fairgrounds. Rushing over multihued rocks and gurgling around deep-banked bends, the river meandered in a clean, scenic pathway.

"It's perfect here. Peaceful." Terra relaxed on a fallen tree trunk and leaned back, closing her eyes. The breeze through the willows smelled earthy and fresh. It was the summer smell of Montana.

She felt Whit's breath on her cheek, and opened her eyes to see him leaned over her, a sinewy brown arm braced on either side of her. He was inches away from kissing her. They both knew it.

"You seem more peaceful than I've ever seen you, Terra." His voice was low, intimate. "And more beautiful."

She smiled, blushing. She was shaken by his nearness. It wasn't this gorgeous man she distrusted; it was herself.

He sensed her discomfort and pulled his arms away. His boots crunched as he crossed in front of her to the water's edge. Bending to pick up a rock, he cussed himself silently.

Fool, you've got her scared of you. You moved too fast before. Now she's involved with this Alexx Light. Get out of here before it's too late.

But it was already too late. The sinking sun peeked over the river bank and shot coppery highlights through her hair. Dancing across her shoulders, the breeze lifted strands and waltzed them into a thick, waving mass of disarray. Whit knew he would never tire of looking at her, never get enough of her beauty.

"I really am happy, Whit."

Her answer caught him off-guard, deep within his own thoughts.

"And you're right," she continued. "I am at peace with myself."

A magpie, curious and bold, lit on a stump near them. They turned to watch the black-and-white bird. Against the lush green background of the riverbank, it was a beautiful sight. The bird tilted its head, as if studying the two people.

Whit watched Terra. Wildlife fascinated her. It was, Whit realized, one of the things he loved about her: her respect for all living things.

They watched as the bird hopped down and explored the riverbank.

"Why didn't you tell me you came to the reservation to find your parents, Terra?" Whit broke the silence. "You knew it was important to me."

"I needed to do it for myself, Whit, not for anyone else." *Please understand,* her eyes beseeched him.

"What made you decide?"

"I went to New Orleans to see Willy and Jen and their twins. I guess I realized then that I want to be able to tell my own children something about their grandparents. All of their grandparents," she corrected herself.

So she was thinking of children. Things with Alexx Light must've progressed quickly. Whit swore under his breath.

"When did you meet Alexx?" It killed him, asking her about her boyfriend, but he couldn't stop himself.

"The first time I came down to Grandmother's house, I stayed for the weekend, and when I got ready to go home, my truck wouldn't start. Alexx lives over the hill from Grandmother. He took me back, all the way home."

"You forgot me awfully fast, Terra." Whit's jaw clamped shut. There was something both hurting and challenging in the depth of his dark eyes. His face was like stone.

Terra began to pace, her arms wrapped around herself defensively. "How can you say that, Whit? There hasn't been an hour since you left my condo after the Powwow that I haven't thought of you."

"Then why didn't you call me?"

"Because I don't want a relationship based on conditions. When you set the rules that I have to live by, you're taking away my control of my life. I need to have choices and make some of my own decisions, no matter how much I love a man.''

Whit snorted contemptuously. ''And does Alexx allow you those choices?''

Terra continued to pace. Whitman Bull Chief might be the handsomest, most intelligent, most fascinating man she'd ever met, but by golly, he was also the most infuriating!

''Why do you keep dragging Alexx into this?''

''Because . . .'' Whit aimed a rock at a branch floating in the river. It ricocheted off the limb, splashing into the water.

''. . . because?'' Terra prompted him.

''Because I can't figure out how you could tell me just a few months ago that you love me, and now it's plain to everybody around here''—he swept his arm to include the fairgrounds and the general vicinity—''that you love him.''

''You're talking apples and oranges, Whit. The love I had . . .'' Terra started over, rephrasing it, ''When I told you I loved you, Whit, I was very sure of myself. Sure of what I felt for you. What I still feel for you. But it has nothing to do with the love I have for my uncle.''

''Your uncle?'' Whit was working up to a good mad, and now his line of anger had been interrupted. Had he heard her correctly? ''Your uncle? Alexx Light is your uncle?''

''Yes, he's my uncle. Who did you think he was?''

Whit ducked his head and blew on his fist sheepishly. He felt stupid. And small. Very small.

''I thought he was your boyfriend.''

''My . . .'' Indignation flushed Terra's face. When it hit her eyes, they practically steamed. ''My boyfriend? You thought Alexx was my boyfriend? After I told you I love you? What kind of a woman do you think I am?''

Whit tried to jump in with an answer. He was too slow.

''Do you think I'd wait my whole life for somebody to

love the way I love you, and then turn around and fall in love with somebody else just because the man I love was pigheaded and stomped out of my condo over one stupid disagreement?'' She stopped to take a breath. Venting one's anger was breathtaking work. And she had lots to vent.

''You don't know me very well,'' she growled, looking into Whit's eyes with a glare of sheer disgust.

''I'm sorry,'' Whit conceded. ''I was so afraid of losing you.''

Terra began pacing again, stiff-legged, crunching river rock with each long, purposeful stride.

''Whatever would make you think Alexx was my boy-friend?'' With each staccato word, she jabbed the air with her finger. If Whit were closer, she would've connected with the end of his nose.

Boy, Whit thought, *she's got spirit. There's no denying, the woman's got spirit.*

''I saw him at your condo the night he brought you back from the reservation. The porchlight was on and I saw you give him a hug before he roared off in that fancy sports car.''

''You were watching?''

''I was on my way to see you.''

''About what?''

''To tell you how wrong I was. To say . . .'' Whit's face softened; his voice mellowed. ''. . . that the choice was yours, as to whether or not you wanted to find your birth parents. I was wrong to issue you an ultimatum. It was completely wrong, and I came back to tell you that.''

Bewilderment creased Terra's brow. ''And you saw me with Alexx and jumped to totally wrong conclusions . . .''

''I did.'' Whit's confession was contrite.

Terra stared at the river. In the distance, the drums began their call. The rodeo had ended and dancing had begun.

''I thought you knew me better than that, Whit.''

''I should have.''

"So where do we go from here?" She faced him, her eyes glistening with unshed tears.

Go for broke, Whit's heart told him. *Admit exactly how you feel.*

"I know where I want it to go, Terra. I love you. I want us to be together for the rest of our lives." He reached for her hand and traced her fingertips with his lips. "I've been miserable without you. My world isn't complete if you're not in it. That's why my supervisor moved up my transfer. He could see I wasn't happy in Washington anymore. My heart wasn't in it. He couldn't wait for me to get back to Montana so he wouldn't have to put up with me!"

"You're working here now?" Terra's heart leaped to keep time with the drums.

"My office is in Billings. I'm just about all settled. But I insisted on coming down here for the Crow Fair this weekend. It's a tradition in our family."

"Speaking of family," Terra remembered, "if you didn't know Alexx was my uncle and you thought he was my boyfriend, why did you go back to save him during the race? You were in second place. You could've won."

"I knew there was a bond between you two," Whit admitted. "I couldn't stand to see you hurt. Besides that, even when I thought he was my rival, he's still a human being. I would've tried to save him even if nobody knew it."

"Cold moon honor." Terra grinned at Whit's surprise. "So, when am I going to meet your family?"

Whit held out his hand. "They're probably up at the dancing right now." He tipped her chin up and kissed her gently. "And from all they've heard about you these past months, they're pretty anxious to meet you. If," he added hesitantly, "you want to meet them."

She nodded and tightened her arm around his waist. "It would be my pleasure."

Outside the tepee of the Bull Chief family, visitors caught up on a year's news, played stickgames, and enjoyed the camaraderie of the fair.

"Hey, Whit," his Uncle Bindy called to him, "where'd you find that pretty girl?" The old man's grin was like a piano keyboard, broad and white. His eyes danced as he looked from his nephew to the beautiful Crow woman hand in hand with Whit.

Introductions circled the group.

"My son has told us you are a very special woman." Lynell Bull Chief was an attractive woman of great poise and charm. Reflecting the genuine interest she held in life, her smile was expansive. Her thick, glossy black hair was pulled back and knotted low into a classic chignon. A chambray shirt with embroidery-trimmed leatherwork was tucked into a denim flared skirt. Peaking beneath the hem was the cast mending her broken leg.

"Thank you, Mrs. Bull Chief," Terra acknowledged.

"Where's Father?" Whit glanced around, searching the familiar straw cowboy hat his father traditionally wore to the fair.

Lynell nodded toward the tepee. "He's getting his horsehair belt to show your uncle."

As if on cue, Ellis Bull Chief stepped out of the tepee. An older, more weathered version of his son, there was no doubt where Whit had inherited his lopsided grin and rugged good looks.

"Did you win this lovely lady at the fair, son?" His dancing eyes teased. His voice was melodic with a thick Crow accent.

It was, Terra surprised herself to realize, an accent she had come to associate with peaceful, happy times. The clipped consonants, the subtle inflections, the way the Crow language rolled off the tongue, was soothing to her.

"Dad, this is Terra Bartlett. Terra, my father, Ellis Bull Chief."

"Welcome, Terra." His hand engulfed hers in an enthusiastic shake. "Welcome to the Crow Fair."

How easily she fit in with the conversation, Terra thought afterward. Two of Whit's sisters joined the group, and the talk volleyed from dance contest results to the hailstorm predicted for tomorrow afternoon.

Somebody mentioned the man injured that afternoon in the three-horse relay.

"Alexx Light is Terra's uncle," Whit explained to his family. "Terra was born to Terisa and Raymond Light."

"I knew Raymond Light," Ellis recalled with near reverence. He turned to Terra. "He was a good man. Good with horses and with people."

"Thank you."

Lynell's brows knotted in concern. "I remember reading about the tragedy. But when Whit mentioned you had been adopted from the reservation, I didn't think about the Light baby." After a moment's thought, she brightened the conversation. "How wonderful that you've come back to your people."

"Grandmother and Uncle Alexx have made me feel very welcome. I feel as though I've known them forever."

"In your heart," Lynell pointed out, "you have, my dear."

"Just like you've been in Whit's heart," his sister Marie observed. Her nonchalant grin told Terra the woman had been her brother's confidante. When Whit had spent time with Marie in Billings, he had held nothing back in expressing his feelings for Terra. Marie could see how much they meant to each other.

"Terra and I are going back to the hospital in a little while to see her uncle." Whit spoke to no one in general. It was enough that he was here with his family and with the woman he loved.

Night fell over the encampment. Hundreds of camp lanterns flared to life one by one, dotting the landscape with flickering flames licking the darkness.

They walked slowly to the car, arm in arm. The moon danced from treetop to treetop, leaving silver leaves in its wake.

"This has been so wonderful." Terra's face glowed. "I'll hate to leave tomorrow."

Whit planted a light kiss on the top of her head. "There'll always be another Crow Fair. Each year seems to get better."

At the hospital, Alexx was awake watching the news when they defied visiting hours to peek in for a minute.

"So you thought I was Terra's boyfriend." Alexx grinned when the story had been told. "That would explain the sour looks I got from you down at the livestock pens."

Both men laughed. The whole thing seemed ludicrous in retrospect.

"I should've given Terra time to explain," Whit admitted. "Taught me a good lesson."

"She's in love with you, Bull Chief." Alexx's tone was serious. "From the look on her face when she saw you standing there, I could tell. There's no doubt in my mind."

Whit grinned and tightened his hold on Terra's hand. She noticed the ease of his features. "I shouldn't have doubted it either."

"Just the same," Alexx said with a laugh, "I'm flattered that you'd think an old coot like me would attract a beauty like Terra. But actually, Miranda, my intended, is every bit as beautiful as my niece."

Whit's sheepish grin subtracted years from his face. "Love does crazy things to a man."

Alexx reached across the cast on his arm to use his good hand. Gripping Whit's hand in friendship, he smiled and nodded at his niece. "Her happiness is real important to me. You make her happy, and that's all that matters to her grandmother and me."

Leaving the hospital, Terra promised Alexx she'd see them in a month or so.

They returned to the encampment, and walked slowly to Neva's tent. The old woman had left a lantern burning. The tepee glowed golden in the darkness, pleasantly welcoming and homelike.

"I'll see you in the morning before I leave, okay?"

"Sure. Come to Billings next weekend?" Whit posed the question tentatively.

Terra nodded. "You bet. I want to see your condo."

"I want to see you." His eyes in the blackness were shining.

The morning's sun found campers stacking tepee poles on the back of flatbed trailers and folding aluminum lawn chairs into the beds of pickup trucks. Another Crow Fair had drawn to a close. By late afternoon, the fairground was empty and silent. Only the ghosts of past dances skipped across the dusty, sun-kissed ground.

Whitman Bull Chief settled into his job in Billings the way an old dog settles comfortably into a grassy spot under a shade tree. Being back in Montana afforded him more time to work directly with the Indian tribes of the state. Moreover, it allowed him time to see Terra every weekend.

Summer days gradually slipped into that golden magnificence which only autumn in the mountains can produce.

Leaves became copper and nightfall crept in earlier each day. A killing frost the first week in September rendered gardens useless. Early morning jogging required mittens and a stocking cap; woodstoves were stoked to take the evening chill from the air.

The Fish, Wildlife & Parks Department set up mobile check stations throughout the state, monitoring hunters and gathering statistics to determine next year's harvest figures. Deer and elk hunting season had opened.

Terra's days became a blur of orange hunting vests and tagged animals to be counted, checked, and logged.

October's winds blew into November's howling snowstorms. Ski slopes opened and the onslaught of out-of-state vacationers with ski bags in hand inundated the airports around the state.

Christmas found Terra and Whit celebrating with the Bartletts. Willy and Jennifer, with their twins now six months old and starting to crawl, flew in to join the family for the holidays.

January's blue-cold days chewed into the bone and numbed cheeks and foreheads. Windchill factors drove the frigid air down to double digits below zero.

Wheezer Johannson cussed the cold; three days last week his logging equipment wouldn't start and he had to stay indoors. He was like a caged bear, ornery and restless.

In February, the trial of Leon Blatz and Fred Meryl got under way in Federal district court. Tacked onto the charges of abduction and felony theft was the charge of shooting the wolf. Terra and Pam were called to testify in court, forcing them to relive the night of their capture. It was small comfort to the women when both men were found guilty of all charges.

When March blew cold and rainy into April, Pam Craft announced her resignation from the Fish, Wildlife & Parks Department to accept a job in Alaska.

Terra applied for a transfer to the Billings office where she could be part of the grizzly bear recovery plan. And where, if she were to admit it to herself, she could be nearer to Whit.

Terra shivered as freezing sleet pelted the kitchen window. Despite the oven being on with a cake inside, the room was chilly. The ceramic tile floor felt hard and cold under her stockinged feet.

Scooping a load of wood pellets from a sack in the garage, she fed the pellet stove's hopper and turned on the fan. Warmth crept across the living room and displaced the chill in the kitchen.

She pulled the curtain back and looked out on the street again. The city's snowplows were almost useless against these late April blizzards when heavy, wet snow blanketed the streets and weighed down tree limbs and roofs. They were the worst kind of storms, turning the highways to sheer ice and catching motorists off-guard.

Whit had told her he'd leave Billings around seven.

Eight, nine, ten, ten-thirty. He should've been here by now.

Terra turned up the fan on the stove and plumped up the couch pillows. Anything to keep her hands from shaking. It made her nervous, worrying about him driving over the pass on slick roads.

Ten forty-five.

Eleven.

She took the cake from the oven and frosted it. She switched CDs from George Strait to a Crow song collection Alexx had given her. The drums blended with her heartbeat, soothing her.

Eleven fifteen.

When the splash of wet snow in the driveway signaled Whit's arrival, Terra was out the door like a flash to greet him.

"Sorry I'm late."

With that dazzling grin of his, she'd forgive him almost anything.

"I was worried about you."

"The mountain passes have slush a foot thick on top of ice, so it's really treacherous driving. There's only one lane of traffic open on Fairfull Pass." He pulled off his gloves and unzipped his down jacket. His arms wrapped around Terra and held her quietly. She was his shelter from the storm.

"Happy Income Tax Day."

Whit scoffed. "That's an oxymoron."

"I know. But I'm glad you're here," she replied lovingly, thankfully. "Let me take your jacket. And I have something to tell you."

Whit's eyes danced. "That you love me?"

"That, too. But my transfer came through. I start working in Region 11, out of the Billings office, starting June first."

"Hey, that's perfect." Enthusiasm buoyed Whit's voice. "I've got something for you, too."

"What?"

"Hold on. I have to get something from the car. Be right back."

Mincing steps down the ice-encrusted stairs, he retrieved a package from the backseat of his car and returned.

"What is this?" Terra shook the suit-sized box carefully, noting the mysterious swishing sound inside.

"Open it and find out."

She pulled off the lid and folded back the snow white tissue.

"Oh." Her voice was little more than a croon. "It's magnificent."

Holding up the beautifully beaded buckskin dress, she admired the handiwork. The leather was delicate and light; the beads were fine and tightly sewn into intricately detailed designs.

"It's from both our families," Whit explained, "not just from me. Your uncle furnished the leather. Neva helped construct the garment itself, and my mother and sisters did the beading."

Terra swallowed hard. Tears threatened to spill over onto her cheeks as she outlined the roses on the shoulders.

"All the work and time that have gone into this," she marveled.

"And all the love," Whit added.

"I never imagined holding anything so beautiful."

He crossed the room and took the dress from her. His arms gently pulled her against his chest. "Neither did I, until I met you."

"I'll cherish it, Whit. Thank you."

"Will you wear it just for me?" His eyes burned into hers with desire and something more.

"Anytime."

"Will you wear it for the festival after a wedding?"

She blushed. "It's called the reception, Whit."

"It's called a proposal, Terra." His eyes were serious, intense. "Will you marry me?"

Whoever designed these monkey suits, Willy Bartlett thought as he fidgeted with the silk tie pinching his neck, *should be forced to wear one on a hot afternoon.*

His gray tuxedo jacket grew warmer as the sun climbed higher in the cloudless blue sky. He should be accustomed to the heat; New Orleans sweltered this time of the year. But it was the altitude in Montana that brought the sun right down on a person's head. The minute Terra's wedding was over, he vowed, the monkey suit would come off so he could dance at the reception in his jeans and cowboy shirt.

"Got everything?" He called to his future brother-in-law as Whit climbed from the car and started up the sidewalk in front of the church.

Whit slapped the pockets of his smartly tailored tuxedo. "Wallet. Keys."

"Wedding ring?"

"Wedding ring." He grinned.

Willy clapped him on the back. "Well then, let's go get the job done."

The two men took the church stairs in quick strides and walked to the annex where they would await the start of the ceremony.

Mason Bartlett paced. His double-shined shoes hit a squeaky spot in the wooden floor as sunshine fractured by the old stained-glass windows bathed the annex in jewel tones.

Pulling his sleeve back, he glanced at his watch. Twenty-five minutes to go.

He continued to pace. Nancy said she'd come and get him when it was time to escort their daughter down the aisle.

His little girl, a bride. Where had the years gone?

She had been the tiniest baby he'd ever seen, all red-faced and squawking when they brought her home. A shock of black hair stood out in every direction from her tiny head.

"She looks like she's wearing a bath mat on her head," Mason had joked. "Do you think her hair'll always stick out that way?"

Nancy had assured him it wouldn't. And it didn't. Terra had beautiful hair, her dad waxed sentimentally.

It flashed before him in rapid succession now; first grade, roller skates, skinned knees, the first bicycle, barrel racing at the junior rodeo, prom night, college graduation, and the bright young woman in the FWP truck.

It had gone so fast, but so happily, Mason reflected.

Volumes of white tissue fell away as Nancy removed the bridal veil from its box and shook it into place. The fresh flowers holding the tulle veiling released their sweet fragrance as she turned to Terra, holding the headpiece for her.

"This is it." Nancy's voice quivered. Whether she was referring to the last touch for the bridal outfit, or about the turn Terra's life would now take, she couldn't say. Her emotions couldn't be trusted right now, she knew. One word from Terra, and Nancy feared she'd lose her composure.

"I love wearing your gown, Mom." Terra caught her reflection in the mirror. The young woman in the ivory satin bridal dress staring back at her looked glowingly happy.

"You're beautiful, dear," her mother confirmed. "I'm honored that you chose to wear it."

"It's perfect. As soon as the formalities of the reception are over, I'll brush the curls out of my hair and braid it, then change into the buckskin dress for dancing."

"Whit will be pleased."

"So will Grandmother. The sash I'm wearing with it belonged to . . . to her daughter," Terra finished hesitantly.

"It belonged to your mother, Terra," Nancy corrected her. "Go ahead and say it."

Terra crossed the room, collecting Nancy's hands in her own.

"Do you remember when you first told me I was adopted? I was in first grade . . ."

". . . six years old." Nancy nodded.

"I wondered why I looked different from most of the kids at school."

"I remember. You said Rusty Lynde called you a red Indian."

Terra's eyes were bright as she smiled. "I hated him for being so cruel. But when I got home, you explained about my adoption."

Nancy caught her lower lip to quell its tremor. "You had a right to know."

"When I got older, you offered to help me locate my birth parents. Why?"

"Because again, you had a right to know. And I guess, deep in my heart," Nancy added as she blinked back tears, "I felt sorry for the woman who had given birth to you. She didn't know what a beautiful person her baby had grown to be."

"That was so unselfish of you, Mom."

"Maybe so, but it was also terribly scary," her mother admitted.

"Scary?" Terra turned in surprise, her veil clouding around her in ethereal beauty.

The older woman's smile was wistful. "I was almost afraid to take the chance . . ."

Her daughter's quizzical look spurred her on.

". . . the chance that when you found your birth parents, you'd go with them, and your dad and I would lose you. It sounds silly, I know. But it was a possibility we'd have to face. When we offered to find your birth parents, Terra, it was one of the hardest decisions we've ever made. We knew it was the right thing to do, but it was hard."

"And yet," Terra's voice caught, emotion thickening it until it could hardly get out of her throat, "you did it."

"Out of love," her mother answered quietly.

Terra held her tightly, relishing the special bond between them.

"Out of love," she agreed, "and honor."

Nancy stepped outside the door and motioned her husband inside. Mason's eyes reflected his pride and adoration.

"Hi, Dad." The bride smiled. "How do I look in Mom's wedding dress?"

"You're beautiful," he answered simply. "Almost as beautiful as your mother looked when she wore it." His gaze traveled to Nancy and held for a poignant moment.

"Thanks, Dad. Mom. I'm ready."

The spell was broken. Nancy tucked a hanky in her purse and went in search of Willy.

Jennifer quieted the twins one last time and adjusted her bridesmaid's bouquet. She took her place, listening for the first chord of the processional and watching for a nod from Reverend Riscoll.

It was an elegant, simple wedding. Afterward, the guests mingled in the Bartletts' lush garden and watched the bride and groom cut a traditional three-tiered cake.

After the photographer had done her duties and toasts had been made, Terra escaped to the bedroom. The heirloom satin gown, her "something old" and "something borrowed," was lovingly hung on a padded hanger and covered. A quick brush through her ringlets straightened her hair, and Terra's hands flew as she quickly braided it into thick plaits on either side of her head.

Skimming her shoulders and floating down to midcalf, the light buckskin dress caressed her body. The sash, Terisa Light's sash, circled her waist like a mother's embrace.

In the garden, Alexx Light introduced his fiancé to the bride's family. Enjoying the festivities, Neva, with Whit's family, circulated and introduced their friends to Terra's family.

The office staff of the Fish, Wildlife & Parks Department sampled cake and compared stories. Max King stood at the edge of the crowd, beaming. He felt partly responsible for the happiness today. And he couldn't be more pleased.

"This is for you, Brother." Willy touched Whit's elbow and steered him to an area beneath overhanging lilacs.

An elaborately decorated saddle sat on a wooden saddle tree. A traditional gift to the Crow groom from the bride's family, it represented the Bartletts' acceptance and support of the marriage.

Nancy and Mason mingled among the guests, receiving congratulations and good wishes from friends and family.

The Indian singers had arrived. Their drums sat in readiness; their sticks were close by, awaiting their magic.

Whit had his back turned away from the house, laughing with his new in-laws, as his friends from the reservation kidded him about being a married man now.

A hush swept over the crowd like wind on wheat.

Whit turned, and met the object of their attention.

Terra stood in the garden path. Her hair hung in thick, glossy braids. The festival dress of buckskin hugged the curves of her slender figure. Intricate beading covered her leggings and moccasins. But it was her beauty, her serene smile, that captured the notice of the wedding guests.

"You have a beautiful granddaughter, Neva." Nancy's arm encircled the old woman's shoulders.

"And you have a very happy daughter," Neva returned.

Both women were right.

Whit walked toward Terra slowly, matching her smile with his own. Their eyes held a promise their hearts had already spoken.

He took his wife's hand, and together they walked to the garden, where the drums began their song of celebration.